Ask Me To

By

Elizabeth Castle

Prologue

Theodora Landry stood outside the door of Brandon Donovan's office. Now that she was here, about to confront him, she wasn't sure what she hoped to accomplish. She wasn't interested in getting her job back, not that she was sure that was what Donovan, as he had asked to be called when she met him last year, wanted in the first place. His message had been vague, his tone not giving away any hint of his purpose in the invitation. And her dismissal from the company had not been what anyone would call amicable. On top of that, he was the reason she'd been fired.

Theo smoothed her skirt, removing the creases from her climb up the flight of stairs that led to the executive floor. She had not gone home and changed after work, assuming her suit would suffice for the meeting tonight. She had debated what to wear before she left the house that morning but had decided it didn't matter. This was hardly a social call.

When Theo reached the landing and opened the door to glance around, she realized the executive floor was empty. The secretary, a busty blonde by the name of Ramona, was not at the front desk. She'd gazed down the hall. If any of the executives were in their offices, she had seen no sign of them. Lights were off behind all the office windows, and the doors were firmly closed for the night. Donovan's lights were the only ones on.

Intent on getting this meeting over with, Theo strode to his door and knocked. When he didn't respond, she knocked again. Getting aggravated with both Donovan and herself, she opened his office door. It wasn't as if she were an employee trying to impress the CEO. The door was unlocked, and the knob turned easily under her hand. Donovan was not seated behind his desk; no angry words at her intrusion assailed her. She entered the room, the door swinging shut behind her.

The first thing she noticed was the smell in the room. It smelled awful, like nothing she'd smelled before. The second thing she noticed was feet clad in very expensive black leather shoes sticking out from behind the dark mahogany desk. Thinking Donovan must have gotten ill, Theo quickly made her way to where he lay.

It became obvious that Donovan was not sick. Brandon Donovan was dead.

Chapter One

Theo sat in her small office, gazing through the clear glass walls that made up the front of her office. It was odd how she always knew when Jack Warner entered the building. No matter how hard she was concentrating on the task before her, she sensed his presence. To be fair, it was more the shift in the behavior of the women in the office outside her glass walls that hinted at his return. Every single woman in the office was secretly primping behind her cubicle walls. Faces were powdered and lipstick reapplied.

On top of that, Jack was hard to miss. He was six feet, five inches tall. She knew because one of the more forward women in the office had asked him, and she felt it was her obligation to share with the rest of the women. He was broad-shouldered, muscular, and quite possibly the most handsome man Theo had ever seen. With his height, his raven-black hair, and his twinkling blue eyes, he was impossible to miss. This was not a man who would ever blend in with a crowd.

Theo tapped a few more keys on the keyboard, trying to ignore him. It was not easy. Jack wasn't around much, at least not in this part of the building, but when he was, she had a hard time concentrating on her work. From her vantage point, she saw him every day when he passed through on his way in and then out of the office, but that was it. As a senior investigator, he rarely sought out the help of the legal team that kept the company, and the investigators, out of legal trouble. But when he did pass through, she and the rest of the women watched him. In the mornings, she had a view of him from behind, the fluorescent lights gleaming on his hair. She would hide behind her monitor when he came back during lunch so that his observant eyes wouldn't see her watching him.

She had been working for her father, Tom Landry, for the past three months, and every day she paused in her work to admire Jack. Her father owned the exclusive private investigation firm. When she found herself out of a job at the legal firm she had worked at, he had insisted she come work for him. She had hesitated because she didn't want any favors from him. At least, not any more favors. But finding a job had become an impossible task, and she had finally accepted.

She had met Jack before she started working here, and she had to admit that being able to ogle him on his way in and out was as good a reason as any other she had for taking the job. Her dad introduced her to Jack when she had come to one of her dad's weddings. She had met him at the reception. Since then, she had met Jack socially on a few rare occasions when she visited her dad. Even after three months of almost daily exposure, she hadn't been able to stop her immediate, very physical reaction to him, though she was sure she hid it well. Just watching him walk through the office, she had an urge to throw herself against his massive body. She wanted him to catch her up in his arms and kiss her like she was the last woman on earth. She, of course, could never tell him that. And what had become painfully apparent after three months of exposure was that Jack didn't particularly like her.

It was nothing Jack said that made her think he didn't like her; it was his behavior. He flirted with almost every female in the office, from the young receptionist who just had her first child to the middle-aged computer technician who ran the firm's technical support team. It was a friendly type of flirting, but he'd never used his charms on her. He smiled at her when he saw her, but his behavior was quite reserved in comparison to the way he treated the other women. She didn't know if it was because she was the boss's daughter or if there simply was something about her he didn't like. She'd gone over their brief meetings time and again to come up with a reason for his aloofness, but nothing she said or did stood out to her. To be fair, she didn't talk much when they were together, opting instead to listen and hope that he might feel even the smallest hint of attraction to her.

Theo tucked a strand of her thick, unruly, blonde hair back into its tight twist and sighed. Jack had a thing for redheads. She couldn't count the number of single women in the building who dyed their hair red. Theo wasn't quite that desperate to gain his attention, especially since it hadn't worked for the other women in the office. As far as she knew, he never dated anyone in the building. And there was no chance she was going to be the first, red hair or not.

Theo wasn't attractive, at least not in the way men seemed to like. She was taller than a lot of the women in the building. She was five-nine, certainly not small and petite. Her blond hair wasn't a nice platinum shade or a pretty gold.

Her hair was more the color of straw, the dried-out kind. Her body was slim, not curvy or busty. She had the build of an athlete, not a centerfold. And while she didn't know if Jack preferred the centerfold type or not, she imagined he did. What red-blooded man didn't want a curvy, large-breasted female? That was two strikes against her.

Theo tapped a few more keys, then sighed again, her gaze making its way back to the office where Jack was chatting with someone in finance. On top of being blonde and slim, she was mousy. She didn't know how to primp and fuss with her appearance the way the other women in the office did. She could never seem to find the right shade of lipstick, and she became frustrated with blush and eye shadow. Her skin was pale, and makeup always ended up looking very unnatural. She kept her cosmetics to a minimum, simply putting on a little mascara, a little blush, and a clear lip gloss.

On top of that, she didn't know how to dress her body in a way that accentuated her figure. And anyway, how do you accentuate something you don't have? While she worked as an attorney, it had been to her advantage to play down her femininity. Clients were more comfortable with someone who looked the part. Here at her father's firm, her lack of femininity was a disadvantage. Working in the main office area like she did now, she was surrounded by attractive females, all of whom knew the tricks of the trade and used them to their advantage. And when male clients walked through their offices, she could tell their efforts were appreciated. More than one man had checked out the women in the main office area, and a few were bold enough to ask one of the women out. Romance was often in the air.

Theo watched Jack greet a few more people as he headed to the other half of the building where his office was. She let out the breath she'd been holding, happy he was now behind the doors that led to the investigator's area so she couldn't see him anymore. Most likely he'd be in and out during the day, but he usually only lingered and chatted in the morning.

Professionally, she admired Jack. He had started off working for a rival firm in his youth, working his way up. Eventually, he had come to work for her father and quickly became one of the most sought-after investigators the firm had. Jack was very particular about the cases he took; a luxury he'd earned. Her father had mentioned Jack often when they'd spoken on the phone. Theo only lived an hour away, but neither father nor daughter bothered to make much time to see each other, though Theo did pop in every six months or so. Theo's monthly phone call to her father eased her guilt for not visiting him more often. She imagined her father was more than satisfied with their long-distance relationship. He'd never had much time for her growing up, preferring to leave her in the hands of her very capable nanny.

But six months ago, she had walked into his office unexpectedly. She had to give him credit for realizing something was terribly wrong. She wasn't sure if it was her unannounced appearance at his office or the dark bruises under her eyes from lack of sleep. She'd blurted out her problems, and he'd immediately promised to help her. She knew, despite their distant relationship, that she could count on him. He might be a womanizer, might be flamboyant and flashy, but he was still her father. And though she'd done her best to be the opposite, at that moment she appreciated him in a way she never had. She supposed it was his belief in her and his unwavering support that made her agree to work for him. When the chips were down, he was there. She couldn't say the same about anyone else in her life.

Theo turned back to her laptop and got back to the assignment at hand. Twenty minutes later, her father knocked on her door and stuck his head in. "I need you in my office."

"What's up?" Theo looked up at the man who was her father. She looked nothing like him. She was blonde, whereas his hair was a reddish auburn, which he kept in a very short cut. She was slim, whereas he was quite fit and muscular. She was reserved, whereas he was flamboyant. She found it funny she'd ended up taller than him. But then again, he had a thing for tall blonds. Her father was five-seven, which for most men was on the shorter side. His bank account made up for any misgivings the women he dated may have had about being taller than him. And since he tended to favor women with small IQs and large bust sizes, she supposed it didn't matter. If he wanted a woman to be arm candy, then he got what he paid for.

"Jack and I need to talk to you."

The mention of Jack had her spine stiffening and her heart racing. Unwilling to let her father know she was extremely infatuated with his favorite investigator, she nodded, closed her laptop, and scooped it up to take along.

Since she had started here, her father never sought her advice, so she couldn't imagine what he wanted. He had seasoned law experts on staff. She'd been a junior member of the law firm she'd been with. She had specialized in things like wills and powers of attorney. She did an occasional title search and wrote up contracts for real estate deals. Business and criminal law were not her areas of expertise, though she had some knowledge. The only reason she had a job here was because she was Tom Landry's daughter. Everyone in the office knew it. The only reason she had a private office was because all of the legal advisers did. Conversations often needed to stay confidential, and that couldn't be done in an open-air office like this one.

"It must be something pretty sensitive to call me in." She hugged her laptop to her chest, feeling very uncomfortable with her father's serious demeanor. He was generally outgoing and usually enthusiastic about whatever project he was working on. He loved to share whatever that project was with whoever would listen. And as the boss, most everyone would stop and listen. Plus, there wasn't a shy bone in his body.

Tom ushered his daughter into the room, his hand on the small of her back. He nodded at Jack, who then smiled briefly at Theo. He held a chair for his daughter and then took a seat next to Jack across the table.

Theo didn't like the feeling she got as both men watched her. She got a sick feeling in her gut. Her father must have read the papers. "This about Donovan?"

Brandon Donovan had been the head of the law firm where she had worked. Though not an owner or a lawyer, he'd been the firm's CEO. He also had ties to a criminal organization. Theo had accidentally stumbled upon his illegal activities. And when she had told one of the firm's owners, she'd been summarily dismissed, and a libel suit had been brought to bear against her. No one had believed her. Her career had ended up in shreds. No one else would hire her. That was when she'd sought out her father's help. A discreet investigation by her father showed it was quite possible the firm's owners knew and were complicit. He'd warned her to stay as far away from them as possible and to drop her accusations. Since she had no proof she could take to the police, she hadn't had a choice, though she hadn't wanted to let it go. So here she was, working for her father with a lawsuit hanging over her head, and nothing she could do about it.

"I'm afraid it is. Brandon Donovan was murdered two nights ago. An investigation is underway. I have a friend on the force who called me to warn me that the cops would be beating a path to my door soon because of your involvement. And when the police find out about the lawsuit against you, if they haven't already, they'll know you have a motive for killing him."

Theo tucked her hands in her lap. She forgot that her father had connections with several police departments in the state. The paper had not mentioned she'd been the one to find his body, so even if her father had read the paper, he wouldn't know that unless the officer told him.

Theo didn't want to remember that night, but she'd thought of little else in the past two days. Her only distractions came in the form of work and Jack. But once she was home, memories of what she had seen would creep back into her consciousness. Sleep would then be hard to come by. She had been using concealer to try to cover up the dark circles under her eyes. She had been drinking a lot more coffee than she usually did, trying to combat the fatigue that weighed her down.

The police already knew about the lawsuit and her being fired from the firm. She'd spent hours at the police station, being questioned and going over her statement. Eventually, they had let her go but with the usual threats of don't leave town and to stay available. She supposed she was high on the list of suspects.

Everything about that day was stuck in her mind. Normally she went right home after work. She'd been job hunting every night since she'd been fired. Even her weekends consisted of much the same. She did her chores, ran her errands, then scoured different websites for jobs around the country. She had yet to find a job and a place that appealed to her enough to uproot her life. When Donovan had left her a cryptic message on her cell, she had wondered if there was even a remote possibility of getting her job back. She'd had a pleasant fantasy of getting her job back, then quitting and leaving them hanging when she found a new job.

But on that night, instead of going home as she should have, she'd headed out to her old offices. Donovan's message told her to meet him at the office after hours. In hindsight, it probably wasn't the smartest thing she'd ever done, but the office was never really empty, so she wasn't afraid of a confrontation with him. Many of the lawyers and their assistants kept late hours. It still struck her as odd how quiet the office had been that night.

"Perhaps you should call them. Tell them we have

nothing to hide." Theo kept her gaze on her father, trying to ignore Jack's presence. Her heart was pounding already, and his beautiful eyes on her weren't helping.

"I took the liberty. A detective will be arriving this afternoon to talk to me about it. I also called my attorney. You're not a criminal lawyer; I don't want you defending yourself."

"So what's Jack for?" Wanting to ignore Jack but unable to, her gaze settled on him.

"I'm for protection." Jack watched as what little color that had remained on Theo's face drained.

"Protection from what?"

Jack answered. "That's the question of the day. Your father is convinced you could be in danger. And while it's a remote possibility, it is a possibility. I'm the best man to protect you should you need it."

Jack wanted to go to her and take her in his arms. It was an impulse he had a lot around her. Her eyes had darkened, and she'd gone pale when she mentioned Donovan. Normally she had an air of innocence about her, but today all he saw was fear. She always had a shy smile for the people she met, always willing to help someone when they needed it. Theo was different from the other women in the office, different from most women he knew, really. She didn't look at him with hungry eyes, eyes that wondered what he'd be like in bed, right after they wondered how much money was in his bank account. Theo saw him when she looked at him, not the six-five giant male others saw. She always had a smile for him, and her kind eyes drew him. And despite the ugly clothes and habitually scraped-back hair, she was cute. She had soulful brown eyes, and her hair was the color of honey blonde with streaks of gold. If she ever let it loose, he imagined she'd be quite pretty. And her height didn't hurt. He didn't feel like a giant when he stood next to her.

But whatever the attraction he felt, right now she needed Jack the investigator, not Jack the man. It was too bad, too. He'd finally decided he'd had enough tiptoeing around her. He'd only kept away from her because she was his boss's daughter. He'd been getting ready to make a move on her despite that fact, but her father asking him to protect her shot that plan out of the water. She was now essentially a client, and he didn't date clients. Not only was it bad for business, but it could prove distracting and dangerous.

So Jack kept his arms to himself and concentrated on the facts. "We know Donovan had ties to criminal activity, specifically drugs. We aren't sure what organization he was working with, but there is no doubt he was. It could be drugs from anywhere in the world. It's too easy to get drugs over the Mexican border. It's not a lot harder when shipped from overseas, so we can't rule that out. And given the vicious nature of his murder, it was personal. You're the only person who ever came out and accused him of illegal activities."

"And look where that got me? I had no real hard facts, and I didn't witness him doing anything illegal. It was a fluke that the package was delivered to my office by mistake. No one believed me, and I was fired." Theo was having a hard time grasping what was happening. Despite having found his body, it had never occurred to her that she could be in danger. Donovan and the firm had made an example out of her. It seemed punishment enough for trying to do a good deed.

Jack tapped the top of his closed laptop. "The problem is now that he's dead, your accusations may be taken more seriously. What your father and I found in our investigation of Donovan three months ago was enough to realize that whatever Donovan was involved in, it wasn't good. We'll turn what we found over to the police. It may help redirect the attention away from you and back to whoever killed him."

Theo blinked back tears. It was a relief to know that Jack didn't consider her a suspect in the crime. She expected her father to believe her, but Jack had no reason to. "So now what do I do?"

Tom held up a hand to hold off Jack. "First you meet with my attorney and tell him what you know. He's due any minute. You'll talk with him before you talk to the police to go over your statement. Then you will meet with the police here in a private office. Then Jack will take you home so you can pack your stuff. We'll stash you at my house."

Jack interrupted. "I don't think that's a good idea. You're the first place someone would look for her when they can't find her at home. Her being with you could put you in danger, too."

Tom nodded, taking what Jack said into consideration. "You may have a point. I could rent an apartment and stash her there."

Jack shook his head. "If you do that, the apartment could be traced financially back to you, which then potentially puts you in danger."

Tom considered that. "She could stay at your place."

Jack vetoed that idea. "We're too close. When they see she's not with you, I'd be a reasonable next guess. But I do know a place I can take her. I have a friend who's going out of town, and he asked me if I could check on his place while he's gone. Instead, I can take her there. There is no reason anyone would trace me there should someone realize she's with me. I'll call him this afternoon."

Theo listened while the men made plans for her. She was still in shock and was only half listening. Things like this didn't happen to boring, unfeminine attorneys. These things happened to adventurous women, flashy women, women with exciting lives. These things happened to centerfold types.

Theo lifted her head when her father rose and kissed her brow. "I'll meet Davis. He's the attorney. We'll put you in the large conference room."

Theo watched her father leave the room, then faced Jack. "I didn't realize you investigated my boss."

Jack shrugged. "When you brought the case to your dad, he turned it over to me."

"He thinks you're a better investigator than he is." Theo had heard her father tell her often enough that Jack was the best, better than he'd ever been.

"I wouldn't go that far, but he's a bit out of practice. He's been a businessman too long. He wanted someone with experience and someone still active in the field looking into it. Donovan was bad news."

"I still don't understand what anyone would have against

me. Not a single person believed me. Brandon Donovan had a sterling reputation. There were rumors he was going to go into local politics. Had his eye on a future governor spot one day."

Jack opened his laptop and started typing. "That's exactly right. There was no way he was going to let a junior associate at the law firm ruin his career. Immediately after your allegation, he started manufacturing lies about you."

Theo rubbed her brow where her father had kissed it. "He accused me of having an affair with a junior lawyer, and when the affair went sour, I wanted revenge. He said I was under investigation for drug abuse, but that he had no proof, so that was why he hadn't fired me before. He said I was unstable. That I stalked my coworkers. He had no one to substantiate those allegations, but the rumors did enough damage. Then the owners got on board and confirmed the allegations in a secondary meeting with the press, expressing their dismay that an employee would turn on them the way I did. There is not a respectable company in a two-hundred-mile radius that would hire me. Other than my dad."

"Your dad has faith in you." Jack clicked through some web pages, looking for anything on Donovan's murder.

"So other than playing bodyguard, what else do you plan to do?" Theo rose and walked over to stand behind Jack. She tried to ignore the breadth of his shoulders while she gazed over them at the screen. He'd done a rudimentary search on Donovan. There were several mentions of his future in politics, the unfounded accusations leveled against him by one Theodora Landry, and news of his brutal murder. The press was only too happy to print all the gory details. She was happy to see her name still hadn't been released to the press as the one who found him.

"Right now I gather facts. I even gather rumors. I take all the seemingly unrelated pieces and use them to figure out what Donovan was involved in and who he was involved with. Knowing the players is the first step. From there I decide if there is any danger to you or not. It seems an unlikely scenario, but I never rule anything out."

She could smile at that. "At least not until you gather all the facts."

"Precisely." He made a few notes on his laptop, then closed it.

Theo took a careful step back and released the breath she'd been holding. Standing so close to him, smelling the soft scent of his cologne, had her knees feeling shaky.

"I'll come with you when the police question you. Davis is fine to handle the legal stuff, but I want to hear what the police have to say."

Theo wasn't sure of police procedure. "Will they let you stay?"

"You're not under arrest. You're just being questioned. Unless they decide to haul you down to the station for questioning, there is no reason why I can't be in on the interview. You and your father are doing this as a courtesy, and you're doing it voluntarily. And I can answer some of the questions you can't about Donovan."

Theo felt a brief moment of shame. Her father had warned her that Donovan was involved in something illegal, but it had been hard to nail down details. She hadn't wanted the details. By the time she'd sought out her father's help, all she wanted was to be left alone. Her career was in shreds no matter what her father found. But it had made her feel better that he had confirmed what she thought she knew about Donovan. But like the proverbial ostrich, she'd buried her head in the sand.

Jack swiveled in the chair to face her. She was frowning, but some of her color was back. It relieved him that she didn't look like she was going to pass out anymore. When her face had drained of all color, he had hoped she would remain on her feet.

Jack was struggling for something reassuring to say when Tom came back into the room. He gestured for the two of them to follow. Jack pressed a hand to Theo's back and guided her down the hall. She shot him a look of surprise, but she hadn't protested his touch.

Davis Montgomery sat at the head of the table in the conference room. He rose and shook hands with Tom, then Jack. His gaze drifted to Theo, but he didn't extend a hand to her.

Theo didn't know whether to be insulted or not. Instead, she took a seat. Her father and Jack seemed to be running this show, so she felt no need to take over now.

Tom took a moment to explain to Davis what had happened at the law firm and how Theo was involved in Donovan's murder. She shuddered when her father explained that Donovan had been beaten and stabbed. That grisly scene would forever be etched in her memory.

Theo listened patiently for a while, became irritated, then blurted out, "I don't suppose it matters whether I did it or not."

Davis nodded. "No, it doesn't matter to me. It's not usually any easier to defend an innocent person than it is a guilty one, and the result is the same. I do whatever I can to keep you out of jail. Failing that, I do my best to take a plea that lessens the sentence."

Theo squirmed in her seat when Davis didn't so much as glance her way as he mentioned the word jail. Then Davis started asking her dozens of highly personal questions.

"The man your previous employer said you were having an affair with, was there any truth to that?"

"No. I barely knew him. We didn't even work in the same department." Theo answered the question, keeping her gaze off Jack. She'd only had one lover before, and it had been a long time ago. The fact that she spent a good part of each day wondering what kind of lover Jack would be had her face flushing.

"Do you do drugs, or are you involved with anyone who does?"

Theo shook her head at that.

Davis jotted a few notes and moved on. "Have you ever been convicted of a crime?"

Exasperated with his questions, Theo rose, as did her voice. "No, I have not been convicted of a crime. I am not involved with anyone who has. I'm not currently in a relationship. I don't do drugs or sell them. I don't have any enemies. I don't owe anyone money. I have never committed a crime. I don't even have a parking ticket. And I didn't kill Brandon Donovan."

Jack didn't smile at her, but he was proud of her for standing up for herself. She might look like a quiet type, but she had spirit. She was going to need it if she was going to get through the next few weeks. And if he found her flushed cheeks and the passion he sensed in her extremely arousing, he kept it to himself.

Davis wasn't even fazed by her outburst. "Good. I don't want to find any skeletons hiding in your closet that will come out and haunt us later. The police may simply question you about your relationship with Mr. Donovan. They'll probably ask why you were fired. If you're innocent, then they won't have any evidence against you that isn't circumstantial. It won't be enough to build a case against you."

Theo gritted her teeth at the "if" part and dropped back into her chair. She could see her father smiling at her, obviously pleased with her outburst. He was always telling her she needed more fire in her belly. The next words out of her mouth stunned the group. "I suppose this is the part where I tell you that they already questioned me right after I found his body."

Chapter Two

It was Theo's father who found his voice first. "You found the body? Why am I just now hearing about this? He was killed two days ago. And why in the world didn't you come to me?"

Theo didn't have the heart to tell him that it never occurred to her to tell him. Despite the fact that she worked for him, they weren't exactly close. Other than when she'd been fired, she hadn't gone to her father for anything since she was a little girl. She never confided in him about anything, not even when she'd been a child. The only reason she went to him about Donovan after she was fired was that he was a private investigator. Had he had any other type of job, she wouldn't have told him.

Jack brushed Davis aside when he would have interrupted. "This puts a whole new spin on the story. Why don't you tell us what happened?"

Theo found it easier to focus on Jack this time, and not her father or Davis. Her father was seething in his chair, angry red flags on his cheeks. She was surprised he wasn't pacing. "Donovan left a message on my cell phone Monday night. He said he wanted to talk to me about my job. I didn't think the firm was going to give me my job back, but I had wondered if they were going to apologize or something. Maybe drop the lawsuit."

"That's incredibly naive." Tom stood and started pacing the office.

Theo glanced at her dad, then back to Jack. "I know. But I couldn't imagine what Donovan wanted. I thought about not going, but I figured it couldn't hurt. His message said to meet him at the office Tuesday after hours. It seemed safe enough. It was pretty quiet when I got there. I greeted a few people I knew on the main floor but headed upstairs straight to Donovan's office. He had his door closed, which wasn't unusual, but I certainly wasn't going to sit around all night waiting for him. The secretary was gone for the evening, so I knocked on his door. When he didn't answer, I opened it."

When Theo was quiet, Jack prompted her. "When you walked into the room, where was Donovan?"

Somber eyes found Jack's. "He was lying on the floor behind his desk. I could see his shoes. The room smelled awful, so I thought maybe he'd gotten sick. I walked around the room where I could see him. He was almost unrecognizable. His face was swollen and bloody. It looked like he'd been stabbed a few times, and the knife used to kill him was stuck in his chest. It was a bit of a haze after that. I ran from the room, and I remember running across the hall. I went into Mr. Marino's office. He's one of the firm's owners. I used his phone to call the police. Then I called the main desk for security."

Theo dropped quiet; the horror of what she saw was getting to her. Bile rose in her throat, but she swallowed it down. She'd never seen a dead body before, and she hoped never to see one again. It was the gruesomeness of the crime that had been keeping her awake at night. She saw

Donovan's bloodied body every time she closed her eyes. She could see it now.

"Did anyone else know you were going there?" Tom spoke up, his voice now that of an investigator instead of a father.

Theo opened her eyes and cleared her throat. "I didn't tell anyone. I don't have any friends here, so I had no one to tell. And honestly, it didn't occur to me to tell you. I figured if anything came of the visit, I could tell you afterward."

The father surfaced again. "You should have told me. I told you to stay away from him. He was not a man to tangle with."

Jack interrupted. "It doesn't matter why she didn't tell you. What happened next?"

Theo took a deep breath and finished her story. "Security escorted me back downstairs. Then the police came. They did what they do, and an officer drove me to the police department. I told the detective what I told you. I told him about the lawsuit and having been fired. I told him about the allegations I had made against him and why. Then I told him Donovan left me a message, so I went to see him. Then I found him. The police had me on the security camera going into the office, so they know when I arrived. Based on the coroner's initial assessment, I arrived hours after he was murdered."

Davis finally piped in. "Do they have any suspects? Do they know when he was murdered?"

Theo turned her eyes to Jack while she answered Davis's questions. "They didn't tell me much. I do know the preliminary reports say he was probably beaten elsewhere. I overheard the detective on the phone. Whoever killed him followed him and stabbed him in his office. It could be who beat him up, or someone else."

Jack scooted closer and took Theo's hand. He ignored her startled expression. He squeezed her fingers when she gripped his tight. "Your being on the security camera doesn't mean the cops don't think you killed him. You would know the building well enough to bypass security cameras. You probably know the building well enough to sneak up to the executive floor. And you're not a small woman. You could have stabbed him easily. Forensics will give the police an idea of how tall the perpetrator was. Hopefully, they can rule you out that way."

"But why would I be in danger?" Theo clutched his hand tighter.

Jack hated to say it but needed her to fully understand the ramifications of what happened. "It's possible the killer knew you were going to be at the office. You might not have told anyone, but that doesn't mean Donovan didn't. It could have been a setup. And you're the only innocent person who knows what Donovan was involved in. You got the package of drugs and cash, and you were the only one to see them before they disappeared from your office. If the killer is tying up loose ends, you could be in danger. He could even be setting you up to take the blame."

"Which is why you'll spend all of your time with a bodyguard until the guy is caught." Tom rubbed a hand over his face, suddenly feeling very overwhelmed.

Jack released Theo's hand. "When you're not with me, you'll have a bodyguard with you. We'll move your office to this part of the building since it's more secure. There's a nice office next to mine that is not being used. You'll be with me at night, and to and from work. If you need to go out, I'll go with you, or assign someone else to go with you."

Not willing to argue, she nodded. The three men started talking around her again, making plans.

* * *

Theo made it through the second interview with Detective Lowell, the same detective who originally questioned her, without falling apart. This time her father, Davis, and Jack were with her. She didn't have an alibi for the day of the murder, which she sincerely hoped she wouldn't need in the future. The police were sure he'd been killed around three or four in the morning, which would give her a window to drive there, kill him, and drive back in time for work. Many of the same questions were asked again. She imagined the detective was trying to see if her story had changed between her first interview and this one. On the plus side, the interview had been brief, and it didn't seem like he was pursuing her as a serious candidate for murder. A lot of the focus of the conversation had been on Jack's previous investigation into Donovan's affairs. Jack promised to turn his files over to the detective. She had watched with a hint of twisted amusement when the detective shook all three of the men's hands, but not hers.

Jack looked at Theo from the driver's seat. She had been quiet since they left the office half an hour earlier. They were on the way to her apartment, but other than giving him directions, she hadn't said much.

"You're awfully quiet, Theodora. Want to talk about what's on your mind?"

Theo looked over at Jack, surprised by his use of her full name. "I was thinking the detective didn't seem to think I murdered Donovan."

Jack glanced at her, then back to the road. "Given the brutality of the murder, it was most likely committed by a man. A large, strong man. You might be able to stab him, but I don't think you have the strength to beat him the way he was. Donovan would have fought you, and you would have had marks on you from the altercation. I would bet the detective believes the man who beat him is also the man who killed him. It's a bit of a stretch to believe they were two separate men, though, like I said before, it's just as likely as any other scenario at this point."

Theo shuddered. Once she was done being questioned, she had tuned out the conversation Jack had with the detective about the investigation he'd conducted three months earlier. "It's hard to imagine who could have done that to him. Did the detective confirm he was stabbed to death? They didn't say so earlier."

Jack didn't want to tell her that Donovan had been beaten to death if she hadn't picked up on it during the conversation he'd had with the detective. The stab wounds were postmortem, most likely to make sure he was dead, another reason there wasn't as much blood as there could have been. He felt no guilt at lying to her. "I'm not sure. The autopsy will reveal the details of the assault, the stabbing, and the approximate time of death. It's possible that if he was beaten with a heavy object, then the assailant could be female. If it was an object, the medical examiner may be able to determine with what. But females rarely engage in that level of violence, and the police will play the odds that it's a man. A woman would be more apt to simply shoot him or stab him and leave out the beating."

"I suppose I've never given any thought to how I might kill a person. Stabbing them to death doesn't seem like the most efficient way, either."

Jack found he could smile at that. She sounded so sincere. "No, it's not the most efficient way. But murder isn't always about efficiency. In this case, whoever murdered him was sending a message. This is the type of thing the mob does or drug cartels. This is not your average, run-of-the-mill assault turned deadly."

Theo glanced down at her hands, unable to face Jack. "I handled wills, contracts, and real estate deals. I didn't get anywhere near the violent crimes. I don't have the stomach for it."

Jack saw her defeated pose. "It's nothing to be ashamed of. I don't care for investigating violent crimes either. But sometimes it has to be done."

Theo knew Jack was very capable, but she never thought about what someone like him would have seen in his career. "Have you investigated many violent crimes?"

Jack's jaw clenched. "Yes."

When he didn't say anything more, and because his "yes" had been terse, she dropped silent again.

He realized he'd snapped at her for no reason. He didn't want to talk about the violent crimes he'd investigated over the years or the violence he'd seen, but he'd started the conversation. He had no call to take his issues out on her. "I'm sorry, Theo. It's a touchy subject."

She imagined it was. "It's okay. I shouldn't pry. You turn left up here, and it's the first apartment building on the right."

The pair was quiet as they made their way to her apartment. Jack was happy to see she had a decent alarm system on her doors and windows. Though she lived in a nice enough neighborhood, criminals were everywhere.

Theo set her keys down on a table in the entryway and set her purse down on the couch. "Is this really necessary? I know my dad is worried, but I can't imagine why I'd be a target."

Theo leaned up against the couch and faced Jack. Now that she was away from the office and her shock was wearing off, she was starting to feel uncomfortable with the situation. She was glad her dad and Jack were willing to protect her if she needed it, but the reality of what she was doing had started to sink in during the car ride. She was essentially moving in with Jack. And while he might be used to living with women, whether for work or pleasure, she was used to living alone. It had been years since she'd lived with a man. And honestly, she wasn't sure her nerves could take being stuck in close quarters with Jack. He might not be attracted to her, but she was ridiculously attracted to him.

"I can't say whether it's necessary or not. Like I said, time will tell. For now, this is the best option. It's better to be safe than sorry." Jack wandered to the bookcase that was jam-packed with books. Not surprisingly, many of the titles involved her profession. And he supposed it was not surprising, with her law background, the number of thrillers and crime fiction she had stashed among the heavier textbooks.

Theo kicked away from the couch. "So where are we going, then? We're still going to work tomorrow, right?"

Jack's fingers ran along the spines of her books, but he was listening. "We'll stay at my place tonight and tomorrow night. If someone were to come looking for you, it would take time to trace you to me. Then Saturday night we're going to move into a friend's house. He'll be on his honeymoon, and we'll be unofficially house sitting."

"A house?" That didn't sound too bad. Chances were the house would have more room in it than either his or her apartment.

"Yeah." He glanced at her open bedroom door. "Be sure to pack a dress."

That threw her. "Whatever for?"

Jack gave her a grin. "I'm the best man at my friend John's wedding on Saturday. You'll have to come with me."

Theo didn't return his odd grin. Instead, she headed for the bedroom, her heart pounding at the thought of going out with Jack. She'd imagined him asking her out, but none of her fantasies involved him telling her she was going to a wedding with him so he could keep track of her. Though there was excitement in her belly, she also felt some dread. She also wished she could pull a sexy red dress out of her closet, but the reality was she didn't own any clothes that were even remotely sexy.

Theo opened the closet and started pulling clothes out.

All of her suits were hung up neatly in a row, jackets and skirts already paired together. She laid those on the bed, then dug into the back of her closet. She had one dress. It was black, ankle-length, and severely out of style. She added it to the pile.

Jack stood in her bedroom doorway, watching as she pulled out one plain suit after another. Theo had no sense of style. He saw the black dress being added to the pile. It would cover her almost as much as a nun's habit.

"Need some help?"

Theo tugged a suitcase out from under her bed. "No. I just need to grab some jeans and shirts for after work and the usual undergarments."

Jack didn't take no for an answer; instead, he came over to where she stood, pulling the garment bag from her. He started with the dress, then layered the suits. He saw her shrug and head for her dresser. Not surprisingly, she was neat as a pin. From what he could tell, everything in her dresser drawers was folded neatly and stacked. His socks were just tossed into the top drawer. Of course, he spent a good minute trying to find matching socks in the morning.

Theo kept her back to him as she gathered up her bras, socks, and underwear. She also grabbed a pair of black stockings to go with the dress. She'd also need her black pumps. Not wanting Jack to see her boring, plain, white and beige underwear, she piled her jeans on top before transferring everything to her suitcase.

It didn't take much longer to grab her slippers, running shoes, and her pumps. She was already wearing her work shoes. She tossed in some nightgowns and a couple of pairs of sweats for good measure. Hopefully, she'd only be gone a week or two. As an afterthought, she went to the bathroom and piled some makeup into her travel case and grabbed her flat iron.

"That was fast."

Theo glanced over at Jack, who now held her suitcase and garment bag. He'd sounded impressed. "I think I'm all set."

The drive to Jack's apartment was silent. Theo couldn't think of anything to say. She'd just packed up her belongings to spend the next couple of weeks living with the most attractive man she'd ever met. And though she managed to have coherent conversations with Jack, they were a strain sometimes. She was too tired to trade wits with him right now.

In continued silence, Jack led her up to his apartment. Theo wasn't sure what to expect from his apartment, but she was sure it wasn't this. Instead of being a quintessential bachelor pad, his apartment looked like a home. He had throw pillows on his couch, there were curtains hung instead of just blinds, and from what she could tell, he had some fancy appliances in his kitchen. The colors were masculine, mostly browns, but the effect wasn't dark because it was paired with a lot of white and blue. She smiled at the oversized flat-screen television. That was probably the most expensive item in the room.

Jack grinned at where she was gazing. "I watch a lot of sports."

Theo turned her head to see his smile. "So does my dad. His television looks just like this one."

"Yeah, I know. We watch a few games together now and

again."

Theo stopped and thought about that. "You know, you're probably my dad's only friend who isn't female."

"You might be right. Is he still seeing Tiffany?"

Theo nodded. Tiffany was one in a long line of women her father dated. He usually only dated them one at a time, but they switched so often, it was embarrassing. Of course, he'd been married five times, so really the embarrassment should have faded a long time ago. But somehow seeing her father with so many women never got easy. It was one of the reasons they didn't see much of each other over the years. His relationship with Tiffany was going on a year, and for Tom, that was a long time.

"He seems smitten with her." Jack headed toward the back of the apartment with her suitcase.

Theo followed. "I know. I'm waiting for the announcement."

"I hope not. I don't want to go to another one of your father's weddings. I've already been to two."

The first time she'd met Jack had been at one of her father's weddings, so she had somewhat fond memories of the two weddings. The first one Jack had been at was five years ago. That marriage had lasted a year. The second wedding had been two and a half years ago, and that marriage had lasted less. "Don't feel too bad. I've been to all but his first."

"Guess you weren't born then."

Theo laughed and gazed around the bedroom. It was obviously his room. A suit jacket was draped over the arm of a cushy chair. "I can't take your room."

"No other place to put you. You'll be more comfortable spending the night in a bed than on the couch. Besides, I've spent a lot of nights on the couch. It will only be for tonight and tomorrow night. My friend John's house has extra bedrooms for guests."

She had to admit the couch did look comfortable. The brown corduroy couch looked overstuffed and oversized. For a man as tall as he was, she imagined comfort was important to him. Even his bed was a California king. She wouldn't be surprised if his feet still hung off. But she had a giddy feeling in the pit of her stomach at the thought of sleeping in Jack's bed.

"Hungry?" Jack set the case next to his closet, opening it up and shoving his clothes to the side to make room for hers. "Why don't you hang up what needs to be hung and come on out?"

Theo watched as Jack half closed the door behind him. He was right; she'd be more comfortable in his bed. The bed had a checkered blue and brown blanket on it, and the sheets were a solid matching blue. The room had dark brown curtains that looked like they'd block out the morning light. On his dresser were what she assumed were family photos. They seemed to be older photos if Jack's appearance was any indication. He looked much younger in them. One photo was with a man who was probably his dad. Another she was sure was his mother. Jack favored his mom's coloring but had his dad's height. Then there was a third picture with a woman who looked not much younger than he was at the time. A sister? The woman had black hair like Jack's but had dark brown eyes. Her features didn't look like she was related. And the way they were smiling at each other didn't look familial.

Not wanting to pry any further, she opened her garment bag and hung up her suit for work tomorrow and her dress. Everything else she'd just leave in the case. She wouldn't be here long, so it didn't seem worth unpacking. There was a private bath, and she peeked her head through the door. She could smell his aftershave and discreetly inhaled the scent. The room was very tidy and clean, though the counter was cluttered with an assortment of male grooming products. Definitely not a slob. She left his room and headed to the kitchen.

"You're not a vegetarian or anything, are you?" Jack's back was to the kitchen doorway, but he knew the moment Theo entered the space. It was disconcerting how attuned to her presence he was.

Theo didn't have to ask why he was asking. Her dad was an on-again, off-again vegetarian. With Tiffany, he was on again. "No. I generally don't eat red meat, but otherwise, I'm fine."

"Good. I've got chicken and veggies for dinner. I also have some sourdough bread."

"It looks wonderful." She watched as he slid a pan into the oven. He'd been busy while she'd been in his room.

"Dinner should be about half an hour. Why don't you have a seat? Want something to drink?" Jack rummaged through his fridge. "How do you feel about iced tea?"

"Iced tea is great." She'd been half afraid he'd offer her something alcoholic. She didn't think Jack and alcohol mixed.

"So, why Theo?"

It was a question Theo had heard before, though she was amused he asked. She usually just gave people half the version of the story. But for some reason, she felt compelled to tell Jack the whole story. "I was supposed to be Theodore. My dad said the doctor was sure I was a boy. My dad had the name all picked out. Theodore Justin Landry. Instead, I came out and became Theodora Justine Landry. I was named after my dad's dad and my mom's grandfather."

"Then why not Thea?" Jack set dinner on the table.

"My dad called me Theo because that's what everyone called his dad. The other reason was that my dad was disappointed I wasn't a boy. It was a way for him to hold onto his dream of having a son. My mom hated it. She called me Dora. They fought about it, and Thea would have been a good compromise. But they were never good with compromise. My mom took off when I was six, and I became Theo. Most of my colleagues call me by my full name, but I guess I've always thought of myself as Theo since that was what my dad called me."

Jack saw Theo's face when she said her father was disappointed she wasn't a boy. It held a resigned sadness. She probably had the right of it. From what he could tell, Tom had spent more time over the last five years hanging out with his nephews than he had with his daughter. It was only recently, with Theo's troubles, that Tom even talked about his daughter.

"I think Theodora is a pretty name. It's unique. I don't think I've ever met another one."

Theo gave him a shy smile and dished up a plate. She

never realized he could be sweet. "I like it. I can't say I cared for being called 'Dora' though. It just doesn't seem to fit me the way Theo does."

Jack was taken aback for a moment at the sweet smile. She'd gazed at him through her lashes, a very feminine look of appreciation in her eyes. He felt a bit dazed and more than a little aroused. He'd purposely not spent much time in her presence because of the effect she had on his emotions, not to mention his body. The body was easy. Despite the ugly clothes and hairdo, she was attractive. She had a slim, not overly curvy body but still had a very feminine shape. She wasn't busty, but she made up for it in the back. He'd spent an inordinate amount of time looking at the way a skirt hugged her butt when she leaned over. And when she wore slacks, his fingers itched to trace those curves.

But with the emotions he was having, he was having a hard time dealing with his body's reaction. He felt a combination of lust, compassion, and protectiveness. It was a heady mix in his bloodstream. And here she was, seated across from him at the dinner table, his table, and he was struggling to find something to say to her. All he wanted to do was drag her across the table and into his arms. He wanted a taste of her so badly, and he had imagined her in his arms dozens of times. He'd even imagined her across the table from him at night and in the morning, which was also disconcerting.

Theo dropped into silence and concentrated on her meal. Jack looked like he was angry about something. She couldn't imagine what she could have said to make him that way. But she'd learned years ago that sometimes it wasn't hard to make a man angry. Her father, for one, had a pretty quick fuse. And her fiancé years ago had been very much the same. It hadn't taken much to set him off. Thankfully he'd get angry and leave the apartment, and she hadn't had to deal with his temper much. Toward the end of their relationship, he'd spent more time away from the apartment than he had in it.

Theo lingered over her meal, not wanting it to end, despite the quiet that descended. Jack had finished his plate before her, and he'd started cleaning up the mess. Theo struggled for something to say. Desperate, she asked him the same question. "So why not Jackson? I heard my father call you that a couple of weeks ago."

Relieved she finally spoke, Jack answered. "I'm Jackson Andrew Warner, Jr. My dad is Jackson, and I'm Jack."

"I can see where that would be confusing. But I like Jack. Do you see your family often?"

More often than she saw hers, but he didn't want to say that, so he nodded before elaborating. "They don't live too far away. My family gets together one Sunday a month. My mom loves to cook. Taught all of her kids. I don't always make it if I'm in the middle of a case, but I try to visit as much as possible."

Theo was an only child, as far as she knew. She hadn't seen or heard from her mother in over ten years, so she might have siblings she didn't know about. But somehow, she doubted it. And her father never had any more children. The most likely reason was that he didn't want to be permanently tied to anyone else. His marriages were short-lived arrangements, and children are, or at least should be, long-term commitments.

"How many siblings?"

Jack tossed the washrag in the sink and turned to face her. He leaned against the counter, not wanting to get any closer for fear he wouldn't keep his hands to himself. "I have two younger sisters. They are both married. My sister Tanya has twin sons, age 2. My sister Roberta has one of each, 3 and 4."

"Do you have children?" Theo blushed, wishing she hadn't asked.

Jack didn't mind. The blush made his fingers itch to touch again. "No. I think you should be married first, and I've been busy with my career."

"Dad can be a bit of a slave driver. But you seem to enjoy working for him."

"Yeah, your dad can be a royal pain in addition to a slave driver. Reminds me of my father in some ways. They both expect perfection. But we get along. He gave me a job when I had just gotten my investigator's license. He took a chance on me."

Theo thought of all the praises she'd heard about Jack from her dad. "He admires you. In some ways, you're the son he never had."

He didn't hear any envy or jealousy in her voice. She was just stating a fact, or how she saw their relationship. "Maybe, in some ways. I certainly gave him enough grief in my early days."

Theo laughed at that. "Good. He never got any from me."

"The perfect child?" Jack crossed the room and took a seat, careful to tuck his hands under the table.

"I guess I wasn't a troublemaker. And he wasn't around

much. He was always working, building up his business. When he wasn't working, he was with a woman. I had a nanny, though. She would probably tell you I was a handful."

Jack couldn't imagine the quiet, studious woman before him being a handful. And it angered him for her that she'd spent more time with a nanny than her father. "What about your step-mothers? You had a few."

"His first wife after my mom didn't like me. But his second wife after my mom was nice. She had a son my age, but he was autistic, and we didn't spend much time together. My dad didn't remarry again after her for a long time. You met his two most recent wives, but I had moved out by then."

Jack wanted to ask more about the first wife but refrained. She was smiling her shy smile, and he didn't want it to go away. "Want dessert?"

Theo was amazed when Jack opened the freezer and put a couple of ice cream sundaes together. He had nuts, cherries, whipped cream, and three kinds of ice cream.

Jack felt himself turn a bit red when he turned and saw her raised brows. He couldn't remember the last time a woman made him blush. He wasn't sure one ever had. He looked sheepishly at the two heaping bowls. "I have an addiction."

Theo couldn't help the laugh that erupted. He looked like a child who got caught with his hands in the cookie jar. "So I see."

Jack handed her a spoon and dug in. He finished his, but Theo only made it through half of hers. Not wanting to seem like a complete glutton, Jack rinsed hers down the drain, though he wanted to finish it for her.

They retired to the living room, and Jack found a basketball game. Though she didn't have much interest in sports herself, she sat back on the incredibly comfortable sofa and watched him watch the game. For a time, she was able to focus on Jack instead of the situation she had found herself in. Feeling fatigue weighing down on her, an hour later she excused herself.

Theo closed the bedroom door behind her and headed to her suitcase. She pulled out a calf-length nightgown and washed up in the private bath, her senses lingering over the aftershave smell that hung in the air. She looked at the bed and determined Jack slept on the left side. She scooted to the right. With a hand on his pillow and the faint smell of him tickling her nostrils, Theo fell sound asleep. When she dreamed, she dreamed of Jack.

Chapter Three

The wedding went off without a hitch, the couple happy and glowing while they exchanged vows. Jack stood beside his friends, honored to be a part of the ceremony. John was his best friend, and Isabelle was an amazing woman. Jack kept an eye on Theo during the photos, and again during the toast. She found an empty seat in the back of the room, but he could see her watching the festivities while she waited for him to be free.

Jack had stood to the side while the bride and groom shared their first dance, joined them at their table for dinner, and stood nearby while they cut the cake. Jack was pretty sure his obligations as best man were finished, but he had yet to seek out Theo. Now John was standing by his side while Isabelle, a vision in white lace and silk, danced with their boss.

"So, is she the lady?" John Bannon handed Jack a glass of champagne, his gaze on the woman across the room who held Jack's attention.

Jack pulled his eyes from Theo. "Yeah, that's Theo."

Jack had told John about Theo and the trouble she was in. John was more than happy to let them stay in his home while he and his now wife were on their honeymoon.

"Not your usual type." John sipped his glass of champagne, his eyes watching Theo. Jack had a penchant for flashy redheads. She was neither a redhead nor flashy. But there was a quietness about her, something inside that shone through. And despite the black dress that practically covered her from head to toe, she could be quite the looker with a new hairstyle and new clothes.

"I'm just guarding her. I had no choice but to bring her." Jack took a sip of champagne and made a face. "Can't I get a beer or something?"

"Don't try to distract me. You like her." John signaled to a waiter and pulled a glass of beer off the tray, handing it to Jack.

Jack set the champagne down and looked at his friend. John had been living in couple bliss for the last six months. He and his wife had met through work. Jack liked her. Had John not been already half in love with her when they'd met, Jack would have made a move on her. But he didn't poach, and John was too good a friend to lose over a woman. But that hadn't stopped him from flirting outrageously with Isabelle and driving John crazy any chance he got.

Looking at John now, he knew there was no way he'd believe Jack was simply doing his job. "Ok, yeah, I like her. A lot. But she happens to be my boss's daughter. And even if she weren't, she's now a case."

"Don't let Tom scare you away. He thinks you're great and would probably rub his hands in glee that you're dating his daughter. You are dating her, right?"

"No, but I'd been seriously thinking about asking her out before this happened. Like I said, now she's a case. It's my job to keep her safe and protected."

John's eyes looked for his wife and found the dance had

ended, but she was still talking to their boss. His eyes softened when he took her in. "Some rules are worth breaking. I swore I'd never get involved with a coworker again, but in short order, I found myself neck-deep in a relationship I didn't think I wanted. She's the best thing that's ever happened to me. And maybe it's the champagne talking, but you could use a nice woman. The women you date are pretty, but they're not the marrying kind. And the way you're looking at your Theo, I'd say you're already halfway in love with her."

Jack took a large swallow of his beer. "I know. I just can't figure out why. I don't know her that well. We've met on and off over the last five years, but we've never gotten past polite conversation. Despite that, there is something about her that pulls me in and intrigues me. I want her so badly I can taste her."

"Then what are you waiting for? Your duties as best man are finished. You saw me married, got your picture taken with the rest of the wedding party, and gave an awesome toast. Go. Have fun. I'm going to find my bride and convince her to dance with me. I suggest you do the same."

Jack watched John claim Isabelle from the crowd of well-wishers. He'd already hugged and kissed the bride, and John was right; his duties were done. There was no reason at all why he couldn't go take his date out on the dance floor for a spin.

Theo watched as Jack moved through the crowd toward her. He'd been talking to the groom quite intently. Theo couldn't help but stare. Jack's friend wasn't traditionally handsome, but he had the attention of many females in the room. He was blond, muscular, and made quite the impact in his tuxedo. She wasn't immune, though she preferred Jack's darker looks. He was tall, but compared to Jack, he looked short.

Jack took Theo's hand when he reached her. "Want to dance?"

Theo desperately wanted to, but she didn't know how. "I'd love to, but I can't."

"Can't what? Dance?" Jack tugged her toward the other couples. "Sure you can. Just hang on to my shoulders and follow my lead."

Theo thought she'd died and gone to heaven when Jack pulled her into his arms. She wasn't a small woman, but Jack made her feel tiny. The first contact of their bodies was electric; at least it was for her. She could feel her heart racing as Jack slid one arm around her waist and the other took her hand. Theo had no choice but to brace her free hand on Jack's shoulder.

"Just watch my feet and follow." Jack guided Theo into the steps. He watched the lights shine on her hair as she watched his feet. She'd not put it up in the tight bun she favored at work. Though still tied up, tendrils had come loose and softened her face. Unable to help himself, he placed a kiss in her hair, taking in the faint perfume she wore. Without thought, he brought her closer to his body.

Theo stumbled for a moment when Jack pulled her closer, but she quickly found the rhythm again. She was so close to him she couldn't watch his feet. But with her breasts and thighs brushing against him, she didn't care. She longed to tuck her palm against his chest, placing it beneath the tuxedo jacket he wore. And she would have given anything for the hand on her back to slip just a little bit lower.

Jack tried to keep a little distance from her but found it impossible. He pulled her arms up and around his neck, bringing her body flush against his. When she didn't pull away, his hands drifted lower down her back, stopping just shy of the curves there.

"Jack?" Theo gazed up at him. The dance floor was lit enough that she could see his eyes. The lights from the DJ booth shone like stars in their depths. She wasn't sure what she was asking him, but he seemed to know. His head dipped toward hers, his mouth just a hair's breadth from hers.

"Sorry to interrupt." The sound of a woman's voice pulled them apart.

Theo quickly jerked back from Jack. Her eyes flew first to Jack, then to the woman.

Jack gave the woman a wry grin. "You've got great timing."

"Sorry, but John is getting impatient, and I want to meet your friend before he drags me out of here."

Theo finally registered that the woman talking was the bride. She took the hand that was thrust at her.

"Hi, I'm Isabelle. Sorry, I wanted to meet you after I talked to John."

Theo couldn't imagine why, but didn't say so. Isabelle was stunning. She had honey-blonde hair that Theo couldn't help but envy. It tumbled artfully around her shoulders. Her unusual lavender eyes were dancing with mischief. She wasn't quite the centerfold Theo envied, but she was close.

Jack led the trio off the dance floor and saw John waiting off to the side. He led the ladies to where he was waiting.

"Sorry, man, I couldn't stop her." John took his wife's hand and pulled her to his side.

"Nope." Isabelle stood on tiptoe and kissed her husband.

Theo was a little uncomfortable in the group. She was usually the one standing alone at parties. Men rarely asked her to dance, and they certainly didn't try to kiss her on the dance floor. Though Isabelle interrupted, Theo was sure Jack was going to kiss her. She licked her now dry lips and tried to take deep breaths to slow the pounding of her heart.

Isabelle released John from the kiss that had started to get heated and turned her flushed face to Theo. "I want you to make yourself comfortable in our home. John told me what Jack told him about you possibly being in danger. I know how scary that can be."

Theo wondered how this happy, glowing woman would know how scared she was, but didn't want to ask. "I appreciate your letting us stay."

"It might have been awkward with all of us in the house, but you would have been welcome anyway. But this way, we get a free house sitter. Hopefully, Jack gets it all straightened out before we get back, but you're welcome either way."

Theo relaxed a bit. Isabelle seemed genuinely friendly. "Where are you going on your honeymoon? Jack didn't say."

"Hawaii. I've never traveled before, and I thought it looked beautiful. I don't have a passport, and John wanted to go to the beach. Which of course I teased him about since we live near the coast and can go to the beach anytime."

Theo smiled at that. She'd lived in California her entire

life, but she rarely made it to the shore. And she had never been out of the state, not even for college. "I've not traveled before, either. It sounds wonderful. I've been thinking of relocating, and I've been researching places to live. I researched Hawaii and found it was really expensive to live there."

Jack didn't hear much after that. He hadn't realized Theo was looking to move away. But given her current circumstances, it shouldn't surprise him. What surprised him was his reaction. She couldn't leave, not now. He couldn't let her leave now that he'd found her. And if that wasn't enough to scare him, nothing was. He wasn't half in love with Theo; he was all the way there. How could that be?

"Are you all right?" Isabelle asked.

Jack shook himself. "I'm fine."

"You turned pale there for a minute. Does the idea of Hawaiian cuisine make you feel ill?"

Jack saw Isabelle's teasing eyes and was glad she didn't know what he was thinking. He was glad Theo didn't know what he was thinking, either. She might have let him kiss her, but she'd probably bolt if he told her he loved her.

"No, just tired. I think you two should get out of here, and so should Theo and I."

Theo was tired, though she wished she were headed back to Jack's apartment for a night of passion. She could tell John and Isabelle were more than ready to get out of the banquet hall and get their honeymoon started.

"It was great to meet you, Theo. I look forward to getting to know you better when I get back." Isabelle wrapped Theo in a big hug.

Theo was startled when Isabelle hugged her, but she hugged her back. John was grinning at his wife and just gave Theo a shrug.

Jack took his turn, then hugged John. Jack couldn't help but grin at Theo's somewhat shocked expression when John hugged her, too. She'd have to get used to his friends. They'd be seeing a lot of them once they were back.

Theo let Jack settle her into the passenger seat of his car after they said their goodbyes to Jack's other friends. He seemed to know everyone there. Theo gratefully sank into the seat of the large sedan. The seat was almost as comfortable as his couch. She pulled her jacket closer around her and slipped off the heels she wore. Theo couldn't help it when her eyes started drifting closed. It was late, and it had been a long day.

Jack drove through the night, glancing occasionally at Theo as the streetlights on the highway illuminated her face. He had packed up the car before they left, so they were headed to John's house. There hadn't been anything to indicate that anyone was looking for Theo, but it was too soon to be sure. And given the fact that he realized he was in love with her, he would do anything to keep her safe.

When they arrived, Jack hated to wake her but had to. He couldn't carry her and the bags inside. He released his seat belt and leaned over. "Theo."

Theo turned her head toward Jack's voice, but her eyes didn't want to open. "Hmm?"

"We're at John's." Jack stroked her cheek with his finger.

Theo's eyes opened about halfway and saw how close Jack was to her. Still half asleep, she found the words she wanted to say earlier. "I wish you would have kissed me."

"Me, too." Jack fought hard not to crush Theo's lips under his. But she was still half asleep. Sighing, he pulled back and got out of the car. He opened the passenger door and helped Theo to her feet. She swayed a bit but found her balance. He kept her elbow in his hand to keep her steady. He didn't think she'd had too much to drink, but with fatigue from the stress of the last couple of days, he figured the alcohol she did drink had gone straight to her head once she'd fallen asleep.

Theo was barely aware of Jack leading her toward the back of the house. Her impression of the house was that it wasn't that different from Jack's apartment. The two men had similar tastes. She felt a nice, soft mattress hit her back a short distance into the house. She sighed and relaxed. Jack was with her, so she was safe.

Jack watched as Theo fell back asleep. Reaching down, he tugged the pins from her hair, letting it loose. The strands probably fell close to her waist when she was standing. Normally hair wasn't a big turn-on for him, but seeing the tresses loose around her face had his blood heating. He looked down and realized she had walked into the house without her shoes. He brushed a bit of dirt off the bottom of her stockings, debating whether or not he should remove them. He wasn't a saint, and he wanted to see.

Without hesitation, he put his hands under her skirt and found the waistband of her stockings. He realized she didn't have any underwear on besides the stockings. He shuddered a bit as he pulled them off her. And if his fingers lingered a bit on her buttocks and thighs as he pulled them off, well, he was only human after all.

Not trusting himself any further, he pulled the blanket and sheet out from under her and settled her under them. She snuggled further into the bed but didn't awaken. Jack leaned down and kissed her briefly on the lips. They parted slightly, but again she didn't wake. Unsettled, Jack let her be, shutting the light off and closing the door behind him. He crossed to the bathroom and turned on the light so Theo would see it should she awaken. She was in no shape for a tour.

Jack got the luggage and brought it in, but left it in the living room. He wasn't sure he'd get any sleep tonight. He raided John's liquor stash, finding his favorite whiskey inside. He poured a glass and settled into the recliner.

In the quiet of the house, Jack's thoughts turned to the past and the brief time he had with his wife. He had been so young, just nineteen, when they'd married. He'd lost her a few years later. It had devastated him in a way he had never experienced and never wanted to experience again. In his youth, he'd thought he'd met his one and only true love. He'd played at love now and again throughout the years. He had been, after all, practically still a kid when he'd met, married, and then lost his wife. Time had healed some of his heart, but he'd not met a woman whom he wanted to love.

He wasn't sure he wanted to love Theo. The first time he'd met her, he hadn't thought much about her. She'd been quiet, and he'd been at her father's wedding with a date. They'd met and greeted each other, but that had been it. The second time he'd met her had been at her father's next wedding. He had not had a date for that one. He'd spent the first part of the night flirting a bit with different ladies. He didn't let the flirting go beyond harmless. He hadn't been looking for a companion for the night. Then he'd seen Theo and remembered her. He'd gone over to say hello, but he'd felt no urge to flirt with her. Something about her felt different, and he couldn't find the words to tease or play.

There had been something so serious about her. But among that seriousness had been a vulnerability that tugged at his heart. They'd talked about mostly meaningless things. They'd talked about their jobs, neither of which was an exciting topic. She already knew what he did since she was the daughter of his boss. He didn't have much interest in the law, other than to make sure he stayed within its rules. But even with the meaningless conversation, he'd found himself incredibly interested in her. He lost himself in her soft voice.

Her looks hadn't been anything to grab his attention, but he found himself giving her a once-over. She had been wearing a brown dress that night. He remembered thinking to himself, where in the world did a woman find such an ugly brown dress. Her hair had been so tightly held back that he had wondered if it gave her a headache.

But once he'd gotten past the superficial thoughts about her looks, he'd started to see beyond them. Her hair, not quite honey blonde but not quite brown, looked like it might have a wave to it. Her eyes were a pretty brown shade. With little effort, she could be quite lovely. He'd been a bit surprised when he caught himself mentally undressing her. He enjoyed women, but he didn't usually lust after them in public.

Nothing about his encounters with Theo had been

normal for him after that. She'd visited her father on one other occasion, but he hadn't gotten to spend much time with her because he was in the middle of a case. He had been shocked when Tom came to him and told him what had happened at her work. Jack had been more than eager to find out what had happened. He hadn't wanted anyone hurting or taking advantage of her. And when Tom told him he'd given Theo a job, he'd been slightly giddy inside. She made him feel like a teenager again with a crush on the pretty cheerleader. Except he wasn't a kid anymore, and Theo was never a cheerleader.

So what had he done? He'd talked himself out of it. He told himself he didn't have a crush on Theo. She was just different from other women he dated, so that had to be the reason he was interested in her. He told himself she was the boss's daughter, that he had no business lusting after her the way he was. When that didn't work, he had rationalized that it was time to act on his desires and ask Theo out. After all, he was a man, and he couldn't suppress them forever. Then Tom asked him to be her bodyguard. It didn't get more complicated than that.

Jack took another sip of whiskey. Maybe John was right. Maybe some rules were meant to be broken. He'd almost kissed her tonight, which would have crossed that line. And once crossed, it wasn't easy to go back. And once crossed, Jack wasn't sure he'd even want to go back. Then again, asking to be kissed was not the same thing as asking him to make love to her. And if she regretted it, or if things went sour, it would make his job that much harder.

Jack grabbed the throw blanket off the back of the couch

before kicking the leg rest up. He settled into the recliner and clicked off the lamp. Fatigue was now, finally, dragging at him. He didn't have to make all the decisions tonight. He'd worry about it tomorrow. With that, the whiskey kicked in, and he fell asleep.

* * *

Theo moaned a bit at the throbbing in her head. She turned blurry eyes to where her alarm clock should be, but it wasn't there. She jerked upright and looked around. Memory came flooding back. Theo dropped her head in her hands, rubbing her temples. A hangover was not how she wanted to start her week. She had no ability to metabolize alcohol, and last night she was pretty sure she had at least two full glasses of champagne. She rarely finished even one glass because the consequences the next morning were never worth it. But she'd been uncomfortable in the crowd of strangers at the wedding. And since Jack hadn't been able to stay with her the entire time because of his best man duties, she had been left to her own devices. Alcohol had made her feel slightly less anxious. And with the week's stress, it had loosened her up a bit.

Theo swung her feet to the floor as the rest of her memory returned. She remembered dancing with Jack. Sober she would have turned him down. But the champagne had been swirling a bit in her brain. If she closed her eyes and thought back to that moment, she could feel Jack's body against hers. She also remembered that he'd almost kissed her. Oh, how she wished he would have. But it was probably just the romance of the setting, and not real interest, that had him almost kissing her. He probably kissed lots of women. She just wished she could have been added to the list.

But in the new light of dawn, with the romance of the wedding behind them, reality was now setting in. He was only with her because he had been assigned to protect her. Today would probably be spent with her doing nothing and Jack trying to figure out who killed Donovan.

Theo looked around the room, not remembering how she got there. She saw her pantyhose tossed on top of the covers, but she had no recollection of removing them. She also realized, though she was still in her dress, her hair had been undone. She blushed crimson when she realized Jack must have put her to bed.

She glanced around the room but did not see her luggage. This room also did not have a private bath. Sighing, and wishing for a hairbrush, Theo left the bedroom. Hoping to sneak her luggage to the bathroom, Theo peeked around the hall entryway into the living room.

"Looking for something?"

Theo gave a tiny shriek and spun around. Jack was behind her, fully dressed and cleaned up for the day. Horribly self-conscious, Theo brushed her tangled hair back from her face. Jack's hair was still damp, and he was wearing a pair of jeans and a button-up shirt. The sight of his bare feet was strangely arousing, and she couldn't seem to tear her gaze away. She forced herself to close her eyes and then look up. Jack's slight smile had her responding in kind.

"If you're looking for your luggage, it's in the living room.

The bath is across the hall from your bedroom if you want a shower."

Theo stiffened a bit as Jack brushed past her, staring after him. Then she spied her luggage and pounced on it. She hurried to the bathroom and shut the door.

Jack headed to the kitchen where he'd left his laptop. He was trying to erase the sight of a very tousled Theo from his mind. Though a bit tangled around her face, her hair did fall halfway down her back. Her mascara had been smudged a bit as if she had rubbed the sleep from her eyes. All in all, she looked like she had slept in her clothes after a long night. And yet he still found her attractive, even tousled. He just wished he'd had a hand in the tousling.

Jack dug through the kitchen and found the pancake mix. Deciding he wanted something sweet, he mixed up enough batter for the two of them. He doubted she'd eat much; he wasn't sure if she generally didn't eat much or if it was the stress of the situation. Either way, she could use a couple more pounds.

Feeling mostly human again, and her headache slightly under control from the pain reliever she found in the bathroom, Theo stepped into the kitchen to find Jack flipping pancakes. She still couldn't get over how comfortable Jack was in the kitchen. Her father never set foot in the kitchen. He kept a cook and a housekeeper on staff. Her ex-fiancé was very much the same. He made her do all the cooking. She either cooked, or they ate out. Theo had gotten tired of eating out, so she had reluctantly taken over all of the cooking, even though she worked longer hours than he did.

"Hope you're hungry. We'll need to make a grocery run. It looks like John and Isabelle cleaned out their fridge before they left for their honeymoon."

"Starving." Theo walked over to the stove. "You don't have to cook for me."

Jack flipped the pancake and looked at her. She was standing beside him. He could see she was uncomfortable with him again. He had hoped she would be relaxed this morning with him, but that was not to be the case. He shrugged. "I would be cooking for myself anyway. And I prefer to eat my cooking."

Theo started opening cabinets looking for plates. She found them and took a couple out. She then set out on a quest for silverware. Finding it, she set the table. "I don't mind cooking, but you do seem to have a knack for it."

"I think I mentioned my mom taught all of her kids to cook. She studied to be a professional chef, but then she married and had three kids. My dad made enough money to support the family, so she stayed home. But she never gave up cooking. I wasn't thrilled with the cooking lessons when I was a kid, but I'm extremely grateful as an adult."

Theo sat. She thought of her childhood. "My dad hates cooking. We always had a cook. It wasn't until I was much older that I figured out the basics."

Jack set the pancakes on the table. Sometimes he forgot when he was talking to her that she grew up in a wealthy home. Tom Landry had always wanted the best. That included a big house with staff. Now that he was no longer in the field, he even kept a driver to drive him around. Theo seemed so incredibly down to earth; he wouldn't have guessed she grew up privileged.

"How old were you when you moved out?"

"Eighteen. I graduated high school early and left for college that summer instead of waiting until the fall. Dad had just moved one of his girlfriends in, and I just couldn't take it anymore. I needed to get out."

Jack thought about how many girlfriends Tom had over the years he'd known him. It had to be hard on his daughter to have them paraded through her home. Most were not very bright, with their biggest assets on display for all to see. Looking at Theo, dressed in baggy jeans and a baggy t-shirt, he could appreciate her more modest appearance. Her face, a bit of her neck, and her bare feet were the only skin he could see. Oddly he was a bit turned on by the sight of her bare feet. Generally, the only skin showing was her face. Even in the last two days together, she had kept her work suit on until bed. The calf-length skirts and stockings covered her up. He had kept hoping her slacks would make an appearance, but he had been out of luck.

Jack pulled his gaze away from her. "I moved out when I was eighteen, but I didn't go far. I studied law, same as you, until I decided to join the police academy. I was a cop for only two years before I decided that wasn't what I wanted to do." He didn't add that his wife was part of the reason he'd quit. She had been constantly stressed out with worry. He had already decided he wasn't cut out to be a police officer, but he might have stuck it out longer if it weren't for her.

Theo set her fork down. "I didn't know that. My father said he stole you from a competitor."

"He did. I was working as a bodyguard at the time. It was

decent pay, and I liked it much better than being a cop. But I realized from hanging out with the investigators in the firm that that was what I wanted to do. Being a cop had its moments, but I figured out what had been missing when I got my investigator's license. My boss wasn't thrilled with me for wanting to change jobs. I was on a long-term assignment working as a bodyguard. That's how I met your dad. He was friends with the guy I was guarding. After a couple of weeks, your dad offered me a job, and I took it. I learned a lot from him."

"Yet here you are working as a bodyguard again." Theo pushed the plate away. She was stuffed.

Jack looked at her half-eaten plate of food and then his. He'd already packed in a plate full and was working on seconds. "I don't mind working as a bodyguard when the assignment calls for it. And I certainly don't mind making sure you're safe."

Theo looked into his eyes and realized he meant every word. Seeing what she thought was caring in his eyes was disconcerting. She thought he didn't like her. Over the past couple of days, she was beginning to realize she might have been mistaken. But if he liked her, even if not in a romantic sense, why was he so distant with her when he wasn't with the other women in the office? Too embarrassed to ask that question, she brought up the topic she didn't want to talk about.

"So now what do we do? Do we just go about our days like you aren't waiting for someone to attack me?"

"No, I keep digging while keeping an eye out for any signs of danger. I keep digging into everything Donovan was involved in and who he was involved with. The law firm's partners are a good place to start. I would bet good money they knew exactly what Donovan was doing. They probably were either complicit or involved. What can you tell me about them?"

"The senior partners are all related. Two of them are brothers, and the third is a cousin. There are a few junior partners; one of them is also related. Donovan was brought in from the outside to manage the firm a couple of years ago."

"Let's start with the brothers." Jack put the dirty dishes in the sink and came back to sit behind his laptop.

"Angelo Marino is the older of the two brothers. He is a well-known and well-respected criminal defense attorney. He's made the national papers a few times for some of the people he's defended. He has a high success rate, so he has had a few high-profile clients over the years. He's in his fifties with two grown sons. Both of them work at the law firm, but neither are partners yet. The other brother is Nicolas Marino. He's also in his fifties. No children, at least none that work at the office. He was a criminal defense attorney, but he's more interested in real estate than he is in law. He's usually working as a consultant and helps gather investors together for big projects. He spends most of his time going over contracts."

"The cousin?"

Theo rubbed her temple with her fingers but continued. "His name is Arnold Marino. He's in his forties and a bit of a ladies' man. He's a lot like my father. He is a bit flamboyant at times and is not shy. He started as a state prosecutor before joining his cousins' firm. He's more of a mover and a shaker. Strums up a lot of business for the firm. He hasn't steadily practiced law in a few years. When he does, he does high-profile divorce cases. A lot of the women he dates, he has helped with their divorces."

Jack grunted at that. "Sounds like a real prize. Do you have reason to believe any of them are involved in illegal activities?"

Theo shook her head. "No. I can't say that I'm a fan of Arnold, but I have always liked and admired the brothers. They are very successful men. The firm is well known. I was thrilled when I got a job there. It was like a dream come true to get hired there. I had barely completed school and finished my bar exam. I had interned at a different firm, and they gave me a glowing recommendation. I was very green when they hired me, but I had hopes of moving up."

"How did they react when you went to them with your suspicions about Donovan?"

"I went to Angelo. I knew him the best out of the three men, though I can't say I know him well. I was at the bottom of the ladder there, but we had spoken at a couple of company events. I brought the package I received and showed it to him. It was addressed to Donovan, so there was no mistake about who it was for. Inside it were delivery dates that had already passed. There were also addresses that I assumed were drop off locations. There was a small stash of drugs, probably for personal use, and five hundred thousand in cash. I took the time to count some of it out and estimated the rest. I was so flustered. All I could think of was that he must be involved in something illegal. Why else would he get that kind of cash in the mail? I typed in a few of those addresses and searched them. They were in shady parts of town, places a man like Donovan would never set foot in."

"What did Angelo say to you?"

"He said little girls should learn to mind their own business. I argued with him. Told him that Donovan was probably dealing drugs or something along those lines. Mr. Marino threw me out of his office. The next thing I knew, security was at my door. My office was cleared out and I was escorted out of the building. Angelo had kept the package, so it was not in my belongings. The next morning a courier came to my apartment and handed me a copy of the lawsuit the company was bringing against me for libel. I tried to get back in the office, but I was barred at the door. One of my coworkers called me and said she didn't know I had been having an affair with Ted Brookston. Said she thought I had better sense than that. I asked her if she knew I had been fired, and she said rumors were I was fired for using drugs."

"And you didn't hear from any of them again until the phone call from Donovan? According to the timeline, you hadn't gone to the press yet when they filed the lawsuit against your allegations. It didn't take long for the lawsuit to hit the papers when you did go."

Theo rubbed her temple harder. "That was the weird part about the whole thing. I never went to the press."

That got Jack's attention. "Your father never told me that. He must have assumed you did."

"I don't know that we talked about it much. By the time I

came to him for help, it was public knowledge that I was being sued for making horrific allegations against one of the city's finest citizens. I was just glad I lived so far away from my dad that his business wasn't tainted because of me."

Jack was quiet for a moment. "If you didn't go to the press, that means someone at the firm did. Whether it was the Marinos or Donovan, it's hard to say. But why leak the allegations in the first place if you weren't going to the press? It doesn't make sense."

"I figured it was a way to punish me."

"Punish you?"

"Yeah. I mean, as soon as the allegations and the lawsuit made the papers, it was a guarantee that no other law firm in the area was going to hire me. I was an instant liability. I was dubbed a drug addict, a liar, and a stalker. Would you hire me?"

"No, I don't suppose I would if I thought the rumors were true." Jack saw the way she was rubbing her temples. "Are you okay?"

Theo rose. "No, I have a headache. I know better than to drink alcohol."

Jack followed her into the living room. She gingerly sat down on the sofa. Instead of sitting beside her, he stood next to the couch. "Turn your back my way."

Theo glanced up at him but obeyed. She practically moaned when his fingers found the tension in her shoulders. She relaxed under his hands, the gentle massage of his fingers helping relieve some of the tension. When his fingers made circles next to her temples, she leaned into his hands.

"I know this is hard for you. You worked there, so you

have insights about the company and the people who work there that I don't." Jack kept the pressure light, but he could see signs of strain on her face.

"I know. It was just a shock. I never met Donovan, though I knew what he looked like and saw him around the office sometimes. I never accused him of anything to his face. I doubt he even knew what I looked like. To have the senior partner throw me out of his office and have me immediately fired was not how I expected our meeting to end. I take it you didn't find anything on them when you went digging for my dad?"

Jack scooted Theo over and sat next to her, continuing to massage her neck and shoulders. "I did some preliminary investigations on them, but nothing stood out. I had been focused on Donovan. And when I found he had ties to some people who were involved in the illegal drug trade, I just kept focusing on him."

"My dad said the people he knew were involved in drugs and guns."

"Allegedly, yes. There isn't any hard proof. But successful criminals usually have really good lawyers."

"You're thinking of Angelo."

"He's a criminal defense lawyer. He has defended some notorious criminals in his career. It's not a stretch that he became involved in some illegal activities himself. Or that he was paid off to look the other way when his company was used to cover illegal activities. Donovan had never been a CEO before, so that was a red flag for me. He hadn't even been a president, vice president, or held any other significant position in other firms. So why would the Marinos hire him to be their new CEO?"

Theo thought about it. She hadn't realized he had no previous work experience in business or law. It was possible he was high up in a serious drug or weapons cartel, and the firm made a nice cover. "So now that he's dead, do you investigate the firm instead?"

"It's the best place to start. Angelo's reaction to you showing him the package tells me he knew exactly what Donovan was up to. If we can figure out who's pulling their strings, we may figure out who killed Donovan, if it wasn't one of them."

"Do you think the Marinos are the ones responsible for his murder?"

Jack pulled Theo into his arms, her back resting against his chest. "I think it's possible they had a falling out over what you had discovered. The Marinos could have been covering up his activities, or been involved in them, but with that package out in the open, someone outside the circle, namely you, knew something was going on. It's possible the Marinos had Donovan lure you to the office. He kept his message vague enough, but enticing enough, to get you to obey his summons. The Marinos could have set it up so that you found the body, making you a suspect. Or it could have been coincidental, and they didn't know you were on your way. It would have been another twelve hours or more before someone found Donovan in his office if you hadn't been there."

Theo leaned against Jack; any thoughts of pulling away from the comfort of his arms had fled when she closed her eyes and savored the feel of him against her. "Either way, the police are looking my way. But if his murder was about revenge, and it was most likely a man, it doesn't make sense to have lured me there to discover the body. And it isn't in the papers that it was me. I would think if it were Angelo or anyone else in the firm, they would have leaked it if they wanted me blamed."

She was right about that. The Marinos had to know she found the body since she was the one who made the call to both the police and the building's security. But they hadn't told the press. They were suspiciously quiet on the subject of Donovan's death on their premises. The papers were speculating but had no corroboration from the firm. It wasn't as if the Marinos could sweep it under the rug.

Or it could have been that they hadn't expected the body to be discovered. It could be that Theo had found the body before the killer had a chance to remove it. She had discovered the body shortly after six o'clock. The killer would have wanted to wait until much later in the evening when he could have been sure the office was empty. Blood could have been cleaned up and the office straightened, though the police would have searched the office in the event of a missing person case, and traces of blood would have been found. But if no one reported him missing, it could have been a long time before the cops opened an investigation into his disappearance.

There were too many questions to answer, too many variables. Jack rested his chin on Theo's head. Regardless of the answers he found, he would protect the woman who sat trustingly in his arms.

Chapter Four

Jack and Theo spent the next couple of days trying to find out as much about the Marinos and the firm as they could. Theo was now in the office next to Jack's, so he would pop in, ask random questions, then pop out again. Her father came in now and again to check on Jack's progress. Honestly, she didn't know how Jack got anything done with her father constantly interrupting him, but it didn't seem to bother Jack at all.

She had to admit she was glad her father was taking an interest. She did not doubt her father cared about her, but this was the first time she could remember him acting like her father. He hovered over her, asked if she was okay. He asked how she was getting along with Jack. He told her to call him should she need him for anything or just wanted to chat. That alone was such an unexpected offer that she felt tears well up at the sincerity and love she saw in his eyes. When he kissed the top of her head again, as he had in his office a few days ago, she wanted to hug him. She couldn't remember the last time she had hugged her father.

It was around noon on Wednesday when she decided she needed some fresh air. Jack was busy working, whether on her problem or someone else's, she couldn't be sure. She imagined he had other cases to work on besides hers. And with things all quiet, she was pretty sure that having a bodyguard was an unnecessary precaution. She had said as much, but both men had vetoed her going home.

Theo grabbed her purse, checking her wallet. She was tired of being indoors and she needed to get out. She often went out for lunch, and now seemed like a good time. Jack was ensconced in his office and would probably not emerge. Her father was having lunch with Tiffany, so he had left already. She decided to go grab lunch and bring something back for Jack. She had brought him lunch from the cafeteria the last two days and thought they both needed a change. Given Jack's penchant for cooking, she was surprised he didn't bring his own food.

The weather was brisk today, but it felt nice. The sky was cloudy and had been threatening rain all day, but so far, the rain had yet to fall. Spring was fast approaching, and Theo couldn't help but wonder if this would be her last spring here. She didn't know where fate would take her, but with her circumstances what they were, it would most likely be far away from here. She knew she would miss Jack terribly when she left. Spending the last week with him had tested her willpower. She wanted to throw herself into his arms at the dinner table when he set a plate before her. She wanted to drag him to her bedroom at night when she was lying there all alone. And when he'd been massaging her neck the other day, she'd wanted to rise up and kiss him like he'd never been kissed before.

Theo smiled to herself. She doubted she had the power to kiss him like he'd never been kissed before, unless it was naively and without much skill. It had been so long since she'd kissed a man; she had probably forgotten how. Not to mention that she hadn't kissed all that many men in the first place. And those men were nothing like Jack. Jack was in a category all by himself. He was smarter, taller, and more handsome than any man she had ever dated. Everything about him shouted male, and she was pretty sure she wasn't woman enough for him.

Theo turned the corner and headed toward the bakery down the street. They had homemade soup, and if she was lucky, they'd have a nice corn chowder or chili today. And she would pick up a cookie for Jack. One of the things she had learned since moving in with him was that he had a sweet tooth. It was either pancakes dripping with syrup, ice cream sundaes with whipped cream, frosted brownies, or some other sort of decadent sweet. He always looked a bit sheepish when he ate them, but he relished every moment. Theo couldn't help but wonder if he would savor a woman like that.

Theo was happy when she finally reached the small bakery and focused her thoughts on food instead of Jack. She smiled at the familiar faces. She came here at least once a week, as did so many other people who worked in the area. She was happy to find that they had vegetarian chili today. She ordered two bowls of chili, a half sandwich for herself, a full one for Jack, and a large chocolate chip cookie for Jack. She thanked the woman and headed back to the office.

Theo never heard the man who grabbed her from behind when she passed an alleyway. The man's glove completely covered her mouth, cutting off most of her air. He easily subdued her when she began kicking her legs and thrashing about. Theo was not a small woman, but he was taller and stronger than she was.

She felt a knife dig into her ribs, and the low voice in her ear told her to settle down or he'd cut her. She froze at the sound of that voice. The knife he held under her waist-length jacket cut through her shirt and bit into her skin. She whimpered a bit at the pain that stung her back, but she stopped thrashing.

"Tell the investigator to back off."

The voice was right next to her ear. She could feel his breath on her face as he spoke. The knife slid across her skin and dug a little deeper. She felt her blouse dampen. His hand was still clamped over her mouth, so she couldn't scream or even cry out. Suddenly she was freed and shoved up against the brick wall of the building. Her cheek hit the brick, and she felt the skin sting. Before she could take a breath, she felt the man press the length of his body against hers, crushing her against the wall. She felt the knife next to her face as it wiped a tear from her cheek that she hadn't been aware of shedding. She saw blood, her blood, on it. Then she felt the man's hand slide around her body so he could caress her breast through her clothing.

"You tell him to back off or I'll be back for you. Next time I won't be so polite, and I'll cut you where it can be seen. I'll make you scream."

Theo gagged when she felt him press his erection against her and his hand tightened on her breast; then suddenly she was free. She dropped to her knees in the dirty alley, sobbing with fear. She saw what looked like military boots in front of her face as the man ran past her. She got a glimpse of dark hair hanging out from under a wool cap, but that was it. He had gloves on his hands, so she couldn't tell what color his skin was. The alley was dark under the overcast sky, and it was doubtful she could have gotten a good look at him had she gotten the chance.

Theo knelt in the alley, leaning up against the brick wall until her legs stopped trembling enough so she could stand. She saw her purse and the bag from the bakery in the entryway of the alley where she had dropped them. She hurried over and grabbed them before someone took them.

Still in shock, with only thoughts of seeing Jack swirling in her head, she half ran the rest of the way back to the office. She ignored the curious stares as she quickly made her way through the maze of cubicles to the other section of the office where Jack was.

When she reached his door, she knocked. When he responded, she opened the door. "Jack."

Her voice was barely a whisper, but Jack heard her. He didn't look up from the monitor in front of him. "Yeah?"

Theo thought for a moment that she was going to lose it then and there. But she managed to swallow her hysterical giggle. She shut the door behind her. "I brought you lunch. And a cookie."

Jack looked up to smile his thanks. He saw how disheveled she was, and she had what looked like a rash on her cheek. He rose, taking the bag from the hand she had held out. He rounded his desk and took her face in his hand. "Did you fall?"

Theo felt her composure shatter. Tears fell down her cheeks as she shook her head. "A man grabbed me in an alley."

Jack swore, pushing Theo into a chair. He knelt before her. Her tights were torn at the knees, and what looked like a rash were abrasions on her face. "Are you hurt anywhere else?"

Theo nodded, some of the numbness from shock fading away now that she was with Jack. "My back hurts."

Jack carefully tugged the jacket off. When his fingers brushed against her waist, he felt something wet. There was blood on his fingers when he pulled them away. He tugged her blouse out of the waistband of her skirt. There was a small puncture wound and a much larger and deeper cut at least three inches in length. He went back around his desk and pulled a first aid kit out of his drawer. He also pulled out a bottle of whiskey. He poured her a drink and handed it to her.

"What happened? Who grabbed you?" Jack was struggling to keep his temper in check. She knew better than to leave the building without someone with her. But her skin was so pale, and the blood on her had his hands shaking. She could have been killed.

Theo held the drink but didn't take a sip. Jack was beside her, and she kept her focus on him. She struggled against him when she felt him rip the back of her shirt open, but his hand on her shoulder stilled her.

"Let me clean this." He took the antiseptic from the kit and dabbed at the wounds. Blood was flowing freely, and he knew she needed stitches. In the meantime, he cleaned what he could and taped a thick gauze pad to her back to help staunch the blood flow. He ignored her sniffles and kept patching her up. He knew the antiseptic stung something fierce, but it had to be done.

Theo let him clean her cheek, but before he was finished, she broke down in sobs. Jack lifted her from the chair and settled her in his lap. He crooned soft words meant to comfort in her ear. She stiffened for a moment, then relaxed completely and let the tears flow. He knew she would feel better for it. He stroked her hair, pulling the pins she used to keep it up. "We need to get you to a hospital and call the cops."

Theo stirred and slid off his lap. She kept her head down, embarrassed that she'd cried all over him. She felt him rise from the chair. He lifted the hand that still held the drink and urged it to her lips. She took a small swallow before sitting back down.

"Get over to the hospital. I'm taking Theo there now. Call the local police and call that detective who's investigating Donovan's murder."

Theo's head rose at the sound of her name and the word hospital. She hadn't realized Jack was on the phone. "Who were you talking to?"

Jack glanced over at her. "Your father. Let's go."

Theo stood still while Jack took his jacket and wrapped her in it. He took her through the back hallway that led to the parking deck. He was parked closer to the front entrance of the building but didn't want to walk Theo back through the office where people would see her. He kept an arm around her as he guided her to his car. She winced when he settled her onto the passenger seat. He wanted to slam the door but refrained. Now was not the time to vent his anger.

They made good time through city traffic. Theo glanced over at Jack, whose grip on the steering wheel was strong enough to turn his knuckles white. She stayed silent, afraid he might yell at her. She had completely disobeyed his orders, and she had no doubt she would hear about it in great detail.

The emergency room was not that busy, and Jack was grateful. They were ushered into a room. Theo's vitals were taken, and she sat docilely while the gauze was pulled from the wounds on her back. He could see they were still bleeding. The nurse helped her out of her bloody shirt and into a gown. The nurse then finished cleaning up the wound, soaking the wound with saline, and covered it until the doctor was ready to stitch it. Theo remained lying on her side with her back to Jack until the doctor arrived. She flinched a bit when the doctor gave her a shot to numb the area while she stitched her up.

"There. You'll need a tetanus shot before you go. We're also going to have you finish the bag of fluid and give you some antibiotics. Just rest a while." The doctor took her leave.

Theo lay on her side, her back still to Jack. She let a few more tears slip through her lashes, but she vowed to stop crying.

"Where is my daughter?" Tom's booming voice was heard throughout the room.

Jack tugged the curtain back and waved Tom over before he disrupted the entire ER. "She's fine. The doctor just stitched her up. Where were you?"

Tom pulled the curtain closed. "I was at Tiffany's place

outside of town. Took me forever to get here."

Tom walked over to his daughter. "Are you all right, baby?"

Theo opened her eyes and stared at her father. She couldn't remember him uttering an endearment to her before. More tears welled up. "I'm fine. Just scared. Jack took care of me."

He turned on Jack. "And where were you? You were supposed to be looking after her."

Jack heard the suppressed anger in Tom's voice. He knew her father was feeling the same thing he was. And he was right; he was supposed to be protecting his daughter.

"I left the building without him." Theo sat up. She was feeling a little woozy after taking the pain pill the doctor ordered for her.

Tom turned to his daughter, hands on his hips. "You what? Of all the stupid things. I told you that you needed a bodyguard. Look what happened the first time you were alone."

Jack saw Theo pale once more and placed a hand on Tom's shoulder. Tom got the message and backed off.

Tom paced the small room. "Tell me what happened?"

Theo wrapped her arms around her waist. "A man grabbed me when I passed the alley on the way back from the bakery. I wanted to get lunch. Jack was working, and I didn't think there was any harm in it. He clamped a hand over my mouth, and I couldn't breathe. He had a knife. He told me to tell my investigator to back off. He said if I didn't, he'd be back."

Jack could tell that Theo was holding something back.

"We need to know the details. What did he look like?"

Theo shook her head. "I don't know. He kept my back to him. After he grabbed me, he shoved me against the brick wall. That's how my face got scratched. He then held the knife to my face. He said next time he'd make me scream. He released me and I fell on my knees. Then he took off. He had military boots on and a winter cap. He had dark hair under the hat, but that's all I saw."

The trio turned when the curtain opened. The tall blond man around Jack's age showed them his badge. It looked like the local police had finally arrived. "Ms. Landry? My name is Detective Macaulay Quinlan. You can call me Mac. How are you feeling?"

Since it was easier to face the detective than either Jack's questioning eyes or her father's anger, she focused on him. This man seemed friendlier than Detective Lowell, who had interviewed her after she found Donovan's body, and again when he interviewed her at her father's office.

"I'm okay. I needed stitches, and I'm waiting for a tetanus shot. But otherwise, I'm fine."

Mac nodded. He'd get a copy of her medical exam for the details of her injuries. He asked her to explain what happened. He kept his surprise to himself when she first told him about how she had been the one to find Brandon Donovan's dead body. Mac knew the man was an aspiring politician and that he had been murdered. The case wasn't in his jurisdiction, but it had made the national press. He was also pretty sure he remembered reading about allegations brought against him by the woman he was now interviewing. He would follow up with the detective working the case.

He then listened to the tale of the attack. He usually had a pretty good feel for people, and he was pretty sure Ms. Landry was telling the truth. If nothing else, the nasty cut on her back was not self-inflicted. Someone had attacked her. "Was there anything familiar about him?"

"I don't think so."

"How tall was he?" Detective Quinlan jotted down notes.

"Taller than me, but not as tall as Jack. Maybe six feet. I couldn't see his skin; all I saw was his dark hair."

"Do you know anyone who fits that general description?"

"What about the Marinos?" Jack took a seat next to Theo and grasped her hand.

"I guess all three of them would. And Angelo's sons, too. They're all pretty tall, and they all have dark hair."

Detective Quinlan made another note. He knew who the Marinos were and that Brandon Donovan had worked for them. "And I'm guessing half the other employees there fit that description, too. It's not enough to go on. But I can look into it and see if they can account for their whereabouts today. I'm guessing they were all snug in their offices. Anyone could have ordered the attack. People in positions of power generally pay for enforcers; they don't get their own hands dirty. I'll reach out to Detective Lowell and see what he thinks. I can't officially investigate Mr. Donovan's murder, but I can question the men who have a motive for attacking you. I'll also see if any cameras might have caught the attack on film. But if it was in an alley, the chances are slim."

Jack stood and shook the detective's hand. The man seemed competent. Jack pulled his business card out and handed it to the man. "Let me know if you find anything out. I'll do the same."

Mac read the card. The very large man in front of him was an investigator with one of the most well-known agencies in town. Though Mac wasn't interested in the help of a P.I., given the circumstances, he wasn't going to turn him down. "I'll be in touch."

Theo lay back down when the detective left, keeping her hold on Jack's hand. Theo hoped there were cameras in the alley. She would rest easier if the police caught the man who attacked her.

Shortly after the detective left, a nurse came in and gave her the tetanus shot. She flinched but otherwise didn't move. It was another two hours before the paperwork to let her go home came through.

Tom followed Jack as he walked Theo back out to the car, keeping a steadying hand under her elbow. "Take care of my daughter, Jack."

Tom faced Theo, his eyes dark. He gently took his daughter in his arms, holding her to him for a moment. "I love you, Theo."

Theo felt her eyes sting, but she wrapped her arms around her dad. "I love you too, Dad."

Tom let her go, gave Jack a final warning look, and headed for his car.

Jack opened the car door and helped Theo inside. When they were both settled and on their way to John's house, Jack spoke. "You want to tell me the whole story?"

"I told you what happened." Theo closed her eyes, feeling incredibly dizzy from the medication.

"You did, but I have a feeling you left something out."

Theo's head dropped to her shoulder when she turned her head to see Jack better. It was dark out now; the only light was from the dash and the street lamps as they made their way back to the house.

In the dark of the car, it was easier to tell Jack. "He touched me. I didn't want my dad to know."

"Where?" Jack's voice was harsh in the quiet of the car, but there was no help for it.

"My breast. And he pushed up against me from behind. He got off on cutting me." Theo's voice was a whisper, and she shuddered as she remembered the man's touch.

"I'll find him, Theo. I swear it." His hands gripped the steering wheel as he envisioned the unknown man touching his Theo. If he found the man, he'd break him in half.

"That's why I didn't want to tell my dad. He would find the man and beat him half to death for touching me. There was a boy once who got a little physical. My dad punched him and knocked a tooth out."

Jack glanced at Theo. Her eyes were droopy. He didn't bother telling her that a missing tooth would be the least of the man's problems. She needed to rest, and she didn't need any more violence. Right now, he was worried about nightmares and flashbacks, but he would be with her should she need him.

When they arrived at the house, Jack helped her out of the car. Memories from the night of John's wedding tickled his mind. He had wanted to kiss Theo that night more than anything else in the world. He had kept his hands and his mouth to himself that night. Seeing her wobble on her feet, he knew he needed to do the same again.

"How are you feeling?" Jack had Theo sit down on the couch while he locked up the house and set the alarm.

"I'm dizzy." Theo's head spun when she tried to face him.

Jack couldn't help but chuckle at that. "You don't hold your liquor or pills well, do you?"

Theo shook her head, feeling a pleasant buzzing in her body. "I think I'm high."

Instead of helping Theo to her feet, he lifted her in his arms and carried her to her bedroom. He sat her on the bed, pulling a nightgown from the dresser. "Do you need help getting dressed?"

"Hmm." Theo closed her eyes, and she felt her body sway. She quickly opened them back up. "What?"

Taking that for a yes, Jack set the nightgown down. She was wearing his jacket and a bra, but the shirt had been discarded. He peeled the jacket off but left the bra in place. He tried not to notice the swell of her breasts over the plain white fabric but failed. She had toned shoulders and a flat abdomen. Her breasts were fuller than they looked under her clothes, though not large by any means. His fingers itched to trace the exposed fullness of them.

Instead, he tugged her nightgown over her head, careful not to snag the bandages on her back. While she sat there, he unhooked her skirt and tugged it off. He lifted her by the waist to remove the tights. He peeled her underwear off along with them. He tried not to notice the slight flare of her hips and her tight bottom, but that, too, was impossible. She didn't seem to even notice he was peeling off her clothes. Sighing, he reached under the nightgown, unhooked her bra, and pulled it out from under the fabric. He kept his eyes on hers instead of on her thighs.

Jack was about to pull away when Theo leaned forward and kissed him. She missed most of his mouth, but she didn't seem to notice or care. She wrapped her arms around his neck, increasing the pressure of her mouth. Unable to resist the lure, Jack cupped her chin and redirected her mouth fully to his. He kissed her back, keeping the contact light. The taste of her was heady, quickly heating his blood. Not breaking the kiss, Jack lifted her and settled her on her back, her head now resting on the pillows. His fingers cupped her unmarred cheek, drinking in and savoring her taste.

Jack groaned and pulled away. He couldn't take advantage of her. She said she felt high, and she was probably right. Pain medication could be quite potent. Theo's eyes were closed, and her arms were now resting quietly at her side. He lifted her again to pull the covers out from under her and settled her under them.

Jack knew she'd sleep for a while. But when she woke, he knew her back would hurt, and her cheek would probably sting. He also didn't want to leave her alone. She had been badly frightened today, her body violated. Sighing, Jack left the room. He poured himself a drink and headed to the shower. He needed to cool off.

An hour later, dressed only in a pair of sweatpants, he climbed into bed with Theo. She turned to him in her sleep and murmured something he couldn't understand. He gathered her close to the warmth of his body, hoping she would sleep soundly through the night.

Chapter Five

Theo snuggled up to the warmth next to her. She didn't remember turning on her heating blanket, but the bed was so warm she must have. The warmth lured her closer, and she burrowed her cold nose into the warmth.

"Good morning." Jack kissed the top of Theo's head as she cuddled closer.

Theo's eyes shot open. There was a large, naked chest right in front of her face. Her gaze shot upwards and saw Jack smiling down at her. "Why are you in my bed?"

Jack snuggled her closer, tucking her head back to his chest. "What do you remember about last night?"

Memory returned. The attack. The hospital. She remembered being in the car. She remembered being really dizzy. Jack helped her to bed. And she'd kissed him! Unbelievably embarrassed by her forward behavior, Theo tucked her chin to her chest.

Jack chuckled. "I take it you remember everything then." He ran his hand up and down her back, hoping to relax her. She had turned bright red, and he assumed she remembered kissing him at that moment.

"But why are you in my bed?" She couldn't bring herself to look into his eyes.

"Just in case." Jack set her aside and rubbed his eyes as he stood up. He looked down at Theo, who was staring at his bare chest. He couldn't help feeling pleased by her reaction to his half-nakedness.

"In case of what?" Her voice was barely a squeak. Seeing that chest in full view had her insides tingling.

"Nightmares." Jack tossed the covers aside and helped her to her feet. He noticed she winced a bit when she stood upright.

Theo thought about that for a moment. Had she not been doped up, she might very well have had a nightmare. She looked at Jack, her heart swelling. "Has anyone ever told you how sweet you are?"

"Not in recent memory. Most of the people who know me would use less flattering words to describe me."

Theo wrapped her arms around his waist, taking a moment to hug him to her. "Well, you are."

Jack let Theo go when she pulled away, though he wanted nothing more than to pull her back to him and back into bed. But the only times she had shown an interest in him physically were when she was drunk or doped up on painkillers. Sober she kept her distance from him.

It was disconcerting. He was in love with her, something he still had a hard time coming to terms with. But she was distant and nowhere near being in love with him. He had loved his wife, and she had loved him. There had been women since who claimed to love him, but he had not felt the same and ended the relationship before it went any further. Thinking of her rejecting him the way he had those women, no matter how gently he had let them down, made his stomach clench. He wanted, no, needed her to feel what he was feeling. That left him reeling and pulling away from her.

"Why don't you have a shower, and I'll help you change the bandage on your back."

Theo nodded and watched as Jack left her bedroom. He had been smiling at her when he woke, but he had undergone quite the mood change once he'd gotten out of bed. It seemed he couldn't get away from her fast enough.

Theo sighed and went to the dresser to pull out her sweatpants and a t-shirt until it was time to get dressed for work. She didn't want to put on anything tight around her waist just yet.

Jack was finishing making breakfast when Theo joined him. Their meal was quiet. Theo was looking at him expectantly, and he knew he should say something. Nothing was coming to mind.

Theo got up and cleaned their dishes once she was satisfied that Jack was done eating. He certainly had a healthy appetite, not surprising given his size. After putting the dishes in the dishwasher, she turned to Jack. "Are you going to lay into me about yesterday or not?"

Theo's brisk words pulled him out of his heated thoughts about taking Theo back to bed. "I figured there was nothing I could say that you haven't already said to yourself."

Theo snorted at that. "Right. I'm sure you've thought of plenty of things to say. I got off easy with my dad last night, but I figured I'd give you your shot."

"If nothing else, at least you'll be more likely to listen to me and your father. We put you under surveillance for a reason. I wish that I weren't needed, but I'd say we now know someone is watching you."

"What if they are watching you? You're the one out there investigating the murder."

Jack thought about that for a minute. "Given our proximity, I'm guessing he was watching you and found out who I am. It's not a stretch to figure out that I'm investigating Donovan's murder. I've been careful to cover my tracks, but I've been with you constantly since your father found out about the murder."

"What if they come after you next?" Theo suddenly realized she had put Jack in danger.

"I hope they do. I'd rather they come after me than you. Let's get you bandaged up so we can get ready for work."

Theo obediently followed Jack to the bathroom. The doctor had given her some antibiotic ointment to put on the wound and some gauze so she could cover it for a couple of days. Jack motioned her to the toilet, and she took a seat. She trembled a bit when Jack lifted her t-shirt. She couldn't be sure, but it felt like Jack's fingers lingered on her bare skin. But before she could react, he was tearing strips off some tape and taping the gauze in place.

"I'll find him, Theo. He won't hurt you again." Jack tugged the t-shirt back into place. She had trembled at his touch but worried it was out of fear.

Theo took a deep breath. "I guess that means we go over the people at the law firm some more."

"We went over senior leaders, but I'd like to learn more about the sons and anyone else with power in the company. I still think Angelo knew what was going on and that's why he went after you. But we can't know if he's the only person involved or what his role is. We need some solid proof."

"All right. I'll finish getting ready. We've got to get to the office. I've got a meeting at nine, and I know my father will want to grill me about yesterday in more detail."

Jack held out a hand to help Theo stand. "Don't let him bully you. His bark is worse than his bite."

Theo laughed. "If you believe that, then I've got a bridge I can sell you."

Jack laughed in return as Theo left the bathroom and closed her bedroom door behind her. His smile quickly faded. He needed to rethink his plan. Theo was in danger, and the man who threatened her might really hurt her, possibly kill her, if he got near her again. He needed to make sure that didn't happen.

* * *

"So, what about Angelo's two sons?"

Theo glanced at Jack, who had his head still buried behind his laptop. She shifted in her chair, finding it impossible to get comfortable. The cuts on her back still hurt, but she refused to take another pain pill. She would make do with over-the-counter pain meds.

"There is Angelo Jr. He is the younger of the two sons. Everyone just calls him Junior. He is the more ambitious of the two brothers. Junior's life goal is to be as good a criminal defense attorney as his father. I would also bet money he wouldn't mind sitting behind the bench one day. His education is extensive, and he's incredibly smart. I don't know him well, but his ambitions are not a secret. He has a bit of an ego problem. Doesn't deign to talk to anyone he thinks is beneath him, and he thinks most people are."

Jack saw her twisting in her seat, and his anger at what happened flared again. Instead of letting the rage go, he turned his focus back to his computer. "The older brother?"

"His name is Marlon, as in Brando. He seems like a nice enough guy. I've met him a few times. He's the less ambitious of the two. I would almost call him disinterested. I got the feeling the only reason he became a lawyer was because it was expected of him. He spends the majority of his time schmoozing clients. He's also a bit of a ladies' man. You rarely see him with the same woman twice. His father wants him to marry and carry on the family tradition, but he doesn't seem to be in a hurry to carry out his father's wishes."

"So, one's a jerk, and the other is charming. Ambition can get in the way of clear thinking and sound judgment. If either of them is trying to live up to their father's reputation, one or both may have gotten themselves into something over their heads."

"If I had to pick who the most likely candidates are, I would say Angelo Senior and Angelo Junior. I can't see Marlon putting the kind of effort into running drugs that would be needed to be successful. But honestly, I just can't see any of them being involved in this. They have too much invested in their firm and too much to lose if they get caught."

"And yet they're the ones who leaked the lawsuit to the press, and Angelo fired you. They certainly didn't want anyone taking your allegations seriously, and they didn't want you around stumbling into any more proof of

Donovan's activities. Or perhaps they also didn't want you around digging further into their involvement, beyond what you learned about Donovan."

"I just don't know. This whole thing is like a bad movie. Things like this don't happen to women like me."

Jack heard an odd tone in her voice. "Women like you? What types of women do these things happen to?"

"Ingénues. Women of mystery. Not boring lawyers."

"You're not boring."

Theo snorted at that. "Tell that to my last date. He couldn't get away fast enough. I didn't mean to talk him to death about why he should write a will. I just couldn't help myself. He has two daughters, and he wasn't thinking at all about their futures should something happen to him. Needless to say, I lectured, and he never called."

"I think it's sweet you cared about the welfare of his children." Jack couldn't help but watch the emotions that played over Theo's face. He supposed many men would find her boring. With her dowdy looks and serious personality, he bet not too many men looked past her looks. They wouldn't appreciate her for who she was.

"I never met them, but he spoke about them a lot. I should have waited until a couple of dates in before bringing up the subject." Theo rose. "Can we go for a walk or something? I can't sit here anymore."

"Sure. We can walk around the office, but I'm not taking you outside any more than necessary. We may stop coming here altogether. It would be better to keep you hidden until we find out who attacked you or who ordered the attack."

She supposed a walk around the office was better than

nothing. She glanced up at Jack when he placed a hand on her upper back but didn't say anything.

"I'm surprised we haven't seen Tom today." Jack guided her to the open hallways, where many of the staff walked the halls to get a little indoor exercise during breaks. Surprisingly, the halls were quiet. A glance at his watch told him it was early yet for the lunch crowd.

"I thought after lunch I'd go find him and get it over with. He won't be happy until he's had a good shout."

"It's his way of working off stress. He would have felt too guilty shouting at you in the hospital."

They dropped silent and simply walked the halls. Theo wanted to take his hand, but that would have been extremely unprofessional. Still, she couldn't help but gaze up at him from time to time.

"See something you like?" Jack meant for it to come out teasing, but somehow it came out seriously.

Theo stopped. She faced Jack, her gaze somber. "Yes. It's hard to hide sometimes. Sorry."

Jack stood dumbly, unable to believe what he'd heard. He watched as Theo quickened her pace, and he hurried after her. "Theo?"

Theo didn't pause but continued on. "Leave me alone, Jack. I need to lie down."

Jack didn't catch her before she closed her office door behind her. He grabbed the door handle and was a bit angered to find she'd locked him out. He figured he had two choices. He could pound on the door and gain the attention of half the office, or he could go back to his own office and work on figuring out who wanted to hurt her. Though pounding on the door was the more appealing of the two options, he went to his office instead.

Theo glanced at the door and was grateful when Jack stopped trying to open it. She didn't know what came over her, or why she would admit to finding herself attracted to him. She certainly had embarrassed herself, and probably Jack. She still remembered the night he'd almost kissed her. And despite the effects of the pain pill, she remembered when she had kissed him. He had pulled back from her instead of taking what she had been offering. Not that she blamed him. He was an extremely attractive man, and she was plain Theo. She didn't even have red hair.

A bit depressed with her thoughts, Theo lay on her stomach on the couch. Since this office was in the executive wing, it had many amenities her regular office did not. There was a fridge, a coffee maker, some nice artwork, and this very comfy couch. She closed her eyes and willed herself not to cry. Fatigue tugged at her, and she fell asleep.

* * *

Jack waited over an hour for Theo to come out. As yet, she had not made an appearance. Unwilling to wait any longer for her to come out, Jack went to maintenance and got the key to her door.

"Trouble in paradise?" Tom lounged outside his office door.

"Your daughter locked herself in her office. I thought it past time to make her come out." Jack held up the key in his hand.

Tom chuckled. "I always worried about Theo. She was always quiet, never had any spunk. Around you, she seems to have found some."

"It's not funny."

"I think it is. So, when are you going to take her out on a real date? You've got the hots for her so bad, I'm surprised you can think straight. I'd think frustration would have gotten to you by now."

Jack's eyebrow rose as he stared at Tom. "Are you telling me you know I've got a thing for your daughter?"

"Well, sure. I've known you for a lot of years, Jack. I've seen that look in your eyes before. Never thought I'd see it aimed at my only child, but I trust you to take care of her and not hurt her."

Jack rubbed his temple. "I don't even know what to say."

Tom chucked him on the shoulder with his fist. "What's to say? You hurt her, and I'll take you out. It's that simple. But you'd be good for her. Get her out of her shell."

"If you take me out, you'll lose your new partner."

"Speaking of which, I've got the contracts back. Have you told Theo you're buying into my firm?"

"No. There's a lot of things we haven't talked about. She doesn't even know I want her. And with my playing bodyguard, now is not the time to let a romance distract me. You know that as well as I do. Besides, she may not want to date her father's business partner any more than she would want to date his top investigator."

"All I can say is that I wouldn't trust her life to anyone else. And if anyone can keep his emotions separate from his job, it's you. Told her about your wife yet?"

Jack shook his head. "No, that's another one of those things we haven't talked about. It's not easy for me to talk about her."

"Theo's got a soft heart. She's a good listener and very understanding of people's softer emotions. Don't know where she got it from."

"She certainly didn't get it from you. You're a hard man, Tom."

Tom didn't take offense. "So are you. But you're not as bad as I am. And by the way, you'll be getting an invitation to my wedding soon. Be sure Theo's your date. Send her to me when you're done. I want to talk to her."

Jack just nodded. Seemed marriage number six was underway. Jack glanced at the door. He wouldn't mind making plans for his second marriage. He just had to work his way past Theo's defenses. After her revelation, he thought it might not be as hard as he had originally thought.

Jack put the key in the door and turned the knob. He was going to tell her how she'd had enough time to sulk, but before he could open his mouth, he saw her asleep on the sofa. She had her arms tucked to her chest, and her face turned toward him. He could see dried tears on her cheeks. He knelt beside her, not sure if he should wake her or let her sleep. He doubted she'd slept much in the past couple of weeks.

Instead of waking her, he pulled his suit jacket off and draped it over her back. He rose, closing the door softly behind him.

* * *

Theo stood outside Jack's door, hand poised to knock. When she woke and found Jack's jacket draped over her, she hadn't known what to think. She didn't want to face him. Didn't want him to feel the need to let her down gently or tell her he just didn't think of her that way. She was his boss's daughter and his responsibility until Donovan's killer was found.

She took a deep breath and knocked. She opened the door when she heard him say, "Open."

"I see you're finally awake. Do you want lunch?"

Theo shook her head and set his jacket on the nearby chair. "I'm not hungry. I'll wait."

"Okay. Your dad wants to see you." Jack leaned back in his chair, keeping his face blank.

Theo wasn't sure what to make of his current behavior, but she wasn't going to argue. She'd rather face her father than Jack.

She strode down the hall and knocked on his door but opened it without waiting for a response. She turned bright red when she saw her father in a clinch with Tiffany. She started to sputter and back out of the room.

"No, don't you leave. Come on in." Tom set Tiffany down from his lap, where he'd been enjoying her company.

Tiffany pouted but got up. "Sorry you had to see that, Theo."

"No worries. I'm sorry I barged in. Jack said Dad wanted to talk to me. I never imagined you'd be here."

"I'd better get going. I've got a long drive back home. Nice to see you again."

"Same here."   Theo watched Tiffany take her leave, closing the door behind her.

"Sorry about that.   Tiffany stopped in unexpectedly." Tom buttoned up his shirt.

Used to seeing her father in a partial state of undress when his girlfriends were around, she simply took a seat and let her father straighten his clothes.

"I don't have much else I can tell you about last night. The man grabbed me, threatened me, cut me, and pushed me. Then he took off. Jack's going over the history of all the Marinos. It's a long history to dig through."

"I have complete faith in Jack. Like I've said, he's the best. What worries me is the fact that you are not taking the threat to you seriously. He could have killed you instead of simply warning you."

Theo swallowed hard. He was right. She hadn't taken the danger he perceived seriously. She should have known. Her father was rarely wrong.

Tom rose and came around. He tugged Theo from her seat, bringing her into his arms. "As a man grows older, he starts to reevaluate his life. I was not a good father to you, Theo, but I want to make it up to you."

Startled by his admission, she pulled out of his arms. A thought intruded, making her stomach clench. "Are you sick?"

"No, just old. Like I said, as you get older, you start to look back on your life and think of all the things you should have done or could have done better."

"You weren't a bad father." Theo knew she spoke the truth. He hadn't been a bad father, just a disinterested one.

"Maybe not a bad one, but certainly not a great one. Come sit." He led his daughter to the couch.

Theo waited for her dad to speak. He seemed serious.

"The first reason I've started reevaluating is because I'm selling half the business to Jack. I'm making him a partner in the business. He's certainly proven his worth, and I'd like to be able to turn over some of the day-to-day responsibilities to him. The second reason is Tiffany. I know this is going to be a shock to you, but she's pregnant."

Theo's mouth fell open. Shock was a mild word for it. She could barely get her response out. "Pregnant?"

"Yeah. She was scared to tell me. And she's even more scared to tell you. That's why she took off so fast. I told her I was going to tell you. I was going to wait until this mess with Donovan was finished, but I figured you'd just get mad at me for waiting."

"Is she okay? Is the baby okay?" Theo couldn't help but think Tiffany was a little old to be starting a family. At forty-two, she was probably her father's oldest girlfriend to date. Her father was only fifty, having been only twenty when she'd been born. She was only two months shy of her thirtieth birthday.

"She and the baby are fine. Her doctor is running all kinds of tests because of her age, but she's doing fine. Shocked and scared, but fine."

Theo wasn't sure what else to say. Of all the things her father could have said to her, that was the last thing she'd ever imagined. Only one question came to mind. "Are you happy about it?"

Tom took her hand. "I am. Tiffany isn't like the other

women I've dated over the years. She's certainly nothing like my other wives, either. I couldn't figure out what it was about her that I found so appealing. Then it occurred to me that I admired her for her mind, among other things."

Theo had not spent much time with Tiffany, though she did like her. She wasn't sure if she was that different from the other women in her dad's life, other than her age. But Tiffany did have a maturity his previous wives lacked, so maybe things would work out. Though not convinced this relationship had a better chance of success than his other ones, she hoped for the baby's sake this time would be different.

"Have you told Jack?"

"No. Didn't have the nerve. I want to get his signature on the contract, and his money in my bank account, before I tell him. Don't want to scare him off. I want to spend time with Tiffany and the baby after it comes. I want to do it right this time around."

"Are you marrying her?" She knew the answer but asked anyway.

"I am. It took some convincing, let me tell you. She didn't want to get married because she's pregnant, and she knows my track record. Said she didn't want to be just another woman in the long line of Mrs. Landry's. She said if she married me, then I'd better plan on until death."

"And?"

"I love her, Theo. More than I imagined I could. I want to love her until death do us part. And I want this baby. If it's a girl, I hope she's just like you."

Of all the things he could have said to her, that shot

through her heart the most. She hugged him tightly. "Thanks, Dad."

Tom patted her back. "Why don't you go on and get Jack to take you home. You look tired."

"When's Jack signing the papers? You don't expect me to keep the baby a secret for long, do you?"

"I think I could convince Jack to sign them today if you really can't keep it to yourself. Why don't you rest here, and I'll go see him. After he signs, I'll convince him to take you home myself."

Half an hour later, her father waltzed back into the office with a big grin on his face. "Signed, sealed, and delivered. As of the first of next month, I've got myself a partner. He's waiting for you."

"Did you tell him?" Theo rolled off the couch, wincing at the stitches.

"Nope, going to let you do the honors. He does know I'm getting married, though. But he also doesn't know I told you I made him a partner. Give you something to talk about on the drive home."

Theo impulsively crossed to her father and kissed his cheek. "I can't wait to buy baby clothes. Bye, Dad."

Chapter Six

They didn't speak much on the way home. Jack did inform her that they would work remotely until Donovan's killer was caught. He was feeling too exposed driving back and forth to the office. And since no one knew where they were, it was safer to stay put.

Theo went straight to the bathroom and pulled out some pain reliever. She headed to the kitchen to get a glass of water. Jack was already there, starting dinner.

"I could get used to having someone cook for me."

Jack set the knife down he'd been using to dice vegetables. He wanted the answers she had denied him earlier. "Someone or me?"

Theo didn't know what to say to that. Instead, she figured it was best to clear up what happened that morning. "Jack, I'm sorry about earlier. I didn't mean to make things awkward."

"You don't know the half of it." Jack turned his back on her and went back to chopping. He needed to work off some of his frustration, and since he couldn't do that with Theo in bed, the veggies were getting the brunt of his temper.

"I know that I'm not your type. I mean, I don't expect you to do anything other than babysit me." Theo dropped her hands to her sides, upset because Jack wouldn't face her.

Jack growled and kept chopping. "Theo, you need to shut

up."

Taken aback by his tone, Theo left the room. She heard Jack slam something on the counter, probably the knife, and was thrown off balance when Jack swung her around. She was even more thrown off guard when he kissed her roughly. His lips were firm, almost punishing against hers.

"I swear, Theo, I don't know how much longer I can keep my hands to myself. You don't think I'm attracted to you? You don't think you're my type? Do you even know what my type is?"

Theo lifted trembling fingers to her lips. She blurted out an answer. "Curvy redheads."

Jack's hands came around Theo's neck, cupping her face. "I've discovered a newly formed desire for tall blondes."

This time when Jack kissed her, he savored her mouth. His temper had faded away as if it had never been. He needed a taste of Theo more than he needed to breathe. He nipped her bottom lip, coaxing her to open her mouth. He felt Theo's hands grip his shirt as she held onto him. He felt a burst of satisfaction when Theo completely opened her mouth to him, surrendering herself to his demands.

Jack's breath was heaving when he finally released Theo's mouth. "We need to talk about this. I want you, Theo. And I think you want me."

Dazed and more than a little confused, Theo dropped her head to Jack's chest. His arms came around her, and she let herself drift for a moment. His big body wrapped around her. When she felt steady, she pushed away. She looked up into his big blue eyes and saw desire there. He did want her. And it amazed her as much as it confused her.

"We don't know each other very well, Jack. How can you know?"

Jack brushed her cheek with the back of his hand. "Some things a man just knows. And I think we know the important stuff."

Theo frowned, thinking of her father. Had he known when he married his wives that his marriages would end? Or had he gone into them thinking that he knew what he wanted? She never asked him. How could Jack be sure she was what he wanted?

"I can see your mind working. What are you thinking?" Jack took Theo's hand and led her back to the kitchen so he could finish dinner.

"I was wondering if my dad knew his marriages would end. How can anyone be sure that what they want now is what they will want later?"

Given her father's history, it was probably not a stretch for her to wonder how sincere he was. He hadn't told her he loved her; she wouldn't accept it if he did. He didn't know how to reassure her. "There are never guarantees, Theo. But I know what I want. I know what I feel."

"Like how you know you want to be a partner in my father's firm?" Theo desperately wanted to change the subject.

"I see he told you. Yeah, like that. I know what I want. I'm not a child. I'm almost forty years old, and I can tell you that I figured out the important things in life a long time ago. And when I say I want you, Theo, I mean for more than a night, or a week, or even a year."

Theo didn't say "forever," and neither did Jack, but it

seemed that that was what he was implying. "I was engaged once. I knew what I wanted. I thought he did, too. But over time, things changed. He realized he wanted something, or rather someone, else. He moved out of our apartment and within six months had married another woman."

"He cheated on you?" Jack tried not to let the shock that she'd been engaged show on his face or in his words. She seemed so untouched.

"No. He left me because he wanted to cheat on me. Once I got over the hurt, I realized he did me a favor. It was better that he left before things went further with his other girlfriend. In a way, it made it a little better. Not a lot, but a little."

"Marriage is serious business." Jack paused for a moment. "And your father reminded me that I should tell you about mine."

Theo almost choked on a swallow of water. "Your what?"

"My marriage. It was a long time ago. It's not something I talk about often. And if I do, I only talk about her with my family."

"What happened?"

Jack tossed dinner in the oven before facing her. "She was murdered."

Theo saw Jack's eyes darken as he remembered what happened to his wife. Her voice was a whisper, and all she managed to get out was his name. "Jack."

"I married her when I was nineteen. We'd been together since we were sixteen. We knew we wanted to get married, but our parents had a fit. They wanted us to go to college. We did school for a while, but then we eloped. We wanted to be married and decided we'd waited long enough. It took us six months to work up the nerve to tell our families. I went to law school for a while, joined the police force, then quit and became a bodyguard. I had told Marnie I wanted to get my investigator's license, and she was pleased. She hated my being a cop, even for that brief time, and wasn't thrilled with my being a bodyguard either. Plus, she was happy I seemed to be serious about getting my license. She never understood why I drifted from job to job. Marnie was always focused, and she was studying to be a doctor. She was incredibly smart and cared about helping people. She was volunteering at a clinic to get some real-life experience. A crazed addict came into the clinic looking for drugs. He pulled a gun. He shot Marnie and two other women. Marnie was touch-and-go for two weeks before she finally died. The other two women lived."

"Oh, Jack." Theo hugged Jack, holding her to him. He had a sheen of tears in his eyes, and it pained her to see them.

"At that moment, I became highly focused on my career. They had the man who murdered my wife, and he went to prison. But it hardly seemed like enough of a punishment. I kept working as a bodyguard for a while. I didn't care anymore about being an investigator. But I knew Marnie would be disappointed if I didn't finish, so I did. Your father gave me a job a year after she was killed."

She remembered when Jack had gotten angry when he'd spoken about all the violence he'd seen. He didn't just investigate crime; he'd been a victim of it. "Is the woman in the picture on your dresser your wife?"

"Yeah. That was taken the day we finally told our parents

we'd gotten married. At first, they were mad we went behind their backs, but then they were just happy for us. My dad took the first picture of the newlyweds. They still have that picture hanging in their family room. They loved her as much as I did."

"How old were you when she died?"

Jack pulled back and saw the tears in her eyes, tears for him. He brushed them away. "I was twenty-four. It was over ten years ago now."

Theo knew Jack was thirty-eight. She thought she knew everything there was to know about him, but she'd been very wrong.

"But I knew at sixteen she was the woman I wanted. I didn't have eyes for anyone else. Neither did she. Losing her taught me to cherish the time we have with those we care about."

Theo absorbed what he said. She wasn't sure she believed him, but he seemed sincere.

The rest of the night, they both were pretty quiet. Jack changed the bandage on her back, and they went to bed early. As far as emotional days went, this topped Theo's list. She wasn't sure where they stood now after that kiss, but Jack didn't seem interested in kissing her again or talking about it. Theo was so tired; despite her nap earlier, she was simply grateful to him for not pushing her tonight.

She slept fretfully and woke up more tired than when she had gone to bed, although she was glad her mind didn't try to relive the attack while asleep. She wasn't prone to nightmares, so she hoped her mind kept it at bay. She thought enough about it while awake that she didn't want it haunting her sleep, too.

* * *

"We've got to be missing something. None of the people at your firm are turning up anything suspicious. No drug problems, no gambling problems, no news articles slamming them in the press. Nothing. You'd think they were saints the way the press talks about them." Frustrated and tired, Jack rubbed the fatigue from his eyes.

"What if it's not them? Maybe they are innocent, and they simply retaliated for what they saw as my attempt to harm the company." Theo had been watching him get more and more frustrated. It had been two days since their kiss, two days of Jack focusing on work, and mostly ignoring her. That in itself was quite a feat since they had stopped going into the office and were now working from John and Isabelle's house.

"Maybe. But if that's the case, I've spent the past two weeks pursuing a dead end. We can't stay cooped up here indefinitely."

Though he had the right of it, part of her wanted this time to never end. Minus the threats, she enjoyed being around Jack. He was smart, witty, and even made her laugh. He also made her feel feminine, something she hadn't felt in a long time. He made her long to buy red dresses and stiletto heels. Of course, she'd probably fall over if she tried to walk in them.

Jack leaned back in his seat. "Maybe I should turn this over to your dad. I just can't seem to find any threads that lead back to who might have threatened you or who might have killed Donovan."

"The police aren't having any luck either. You can't find something that's not there. And I might advise against asking my dad for help. His mind is not on his work."

Jack wanted to tell her his wasn't either, but he didn't want her to lose faith in him. "You wouldn't think marriage would distract him that much since it's his sixth one."

Theo laughed. "You've got that right. But that's not what has his mind in a twist."

"No?" Jack felt himself smile at her easy laughter, despite his annoyance.

"He told me something the other day in the office. He isn't too crazy about everyone knowing about it. And with all that was going on, I wasn't sure if I should say anything or not."

When she didn't continue, Jack pushed. "You can't leave me hanging now that you've tickled my curiosity. Investigators want answers."

"You remember when you asked me if I had any other brothers or sisters, and I said no?"

"Yeah." Jack wasn't sure where she was going with this.

"Well, I can't say that anymore."

Jack sat confused for a moment; then it dawned on him what she meant. "Sweet heaven, your father got Tiffany pregnant?"

"Yes, he did. From what I understand, Tiffany was not looking forward to telling my dad. Or me, for that matter. But she did, and Dad seems happy about it. He said Tiffany and the baby are doing well."

"How do you feel about it?"

"My reaction was about the same as yours. When I was a kid, I wanted a sibling. Looks like I'm getting one."

"Siblings are more fun when you're older. I wanted to wish mine away when I was younger. My sisters used to drive me crazy. Now I miss them when I don't get to see them."

It was hard to accept that a brother or sister was a reality. "I imagine the relationship I have with mine will be a lot different from your relationship with yours. I'm at an age where I should be having children of my own. But at the rate I've been going, I guess children are not in my future."

Jack looked up, surprised to hear her say that. "You're young enough to have children, Theo. Though I can see where it might be a little awkward for the child to have an aunt or uncle not much older."

Theo kept her eyes on the computer in front of her. "Like you, I want to be married before I have children. And I'm almost thirty with no prospects. I guess I just assume things are not going to change in the next few years. I think I've forgotten how to date. And marriage is not something you should rush into. Assuming I do meet someone and get married, I'm not sure I want to have a baby when I'm almost forty."

"I'm almost forty, and I would with the right woman." Jack tipped a finger under her chin. "A prospect might be closer than you think."

Theo saw the seriousness in his gaze. "Jack, I wish you wouldn't do that."

"Do what?"

"Say things like that to me. I know you said you were interested, but you can't possibly be serious about a real, long-term relationship between you and me. You don't even like me."

Jack's brow shot up. "Who says I don't like you?"

Theo tucked her hands in her lap, struggling to keep her self-control. "I do. You don't treat me like you do other women."

"No, I don't. And if you think about that a little harder, you'd see it as a sign that I don't think of you like I think of all those other women. I like you, Theo. I happen to like you a lot. You're smart. You're a bit shy, but it's sweet. You're nice to others; you care about people. Look at you and your dad. You could resent him for the way he treated you growing up, but instead, you accept him for who he is. There's a very nice person inside you."

It didn't get past her notice that he said nothing about her looks. "That's what men say about dowdy women. It's not what's on the outside that matters; it's what's on the inside. It's a big crock, Jack. Men are visual creatures. They either see something they like, or they don't. And men don't."

"You tempt me to show you how wrong you are. I've no doubt there are plenty of shallow men out there, women too, who don't look beyond the surface. But I'm attracted to your surface as much as I am to who you are. Women don't generally see past my face and body. You do."

Theo thought about all the times she'd lusted after Jack. How was she different from those other women, other than keeping it to herself? But in some ways, he was right. His looks were a detriment to her. She wanted a normal guy.

Maybe with a bit of a gut or balding; one who wasn't quite so perfect, so she wouldn't feel so imperfect next to him. In her eyes, Jack was about as perfect as perfect could get. And she was far from it.

"Theo, there is nothing wrong with you. You've got thick, soft hair; your eyes are soulful. And if given a chance, I'd like to get you naked." Jack kept his eyes on Theo's, willing her to see what he saw.

"I'm sorry, Jack. I imagine insecurity is not attractive. I don't know how to be like the women you've dated over the years. And I don't understand why you would want me."

Jack had enough. "Theo, come here."

Theo shook her head at him.

"Theo." Jack came around the table, pulling her to her feet. "I think we've gone enough rounds with words. Let's try something else."

Theo could only grab onto Jack's shoulders when he picked her up. The room spun around as he quickly strode down the hall to his bedroom.

"Jack, what are you doing?" The words were barely audible as Jack set her on her feet beside his bed.

"I'm going to make love to you, Theo. Maybe then you'll be able to accept that I have feelings for you. I don't care what you look like. But for the record, I like everything I see."

Theo was startled into submission when Jack's hands grabbed her waist and lifted her against him. She could feel the hardness of his body pressed along the entire length of hers.

"Kiss me, Theo." Jack brought her closer, his mouth a

breath away from hers. Her deep brown eyes were unsure as they gazed up at him. When he cupped one hand behind her neck, she finally gave him what he sought.

Theo closed her eyes and kissed Jack. Though they had shared that amazing kiss the other day, Jack was the one who initiated it, the one who led where it would go. Theo kept the pressure of her mouth light, hoping Jack would show her what he wanted.

"Open your mouth for me, Theo." Jack brushed his lips against hers, no more than a whisper. She was barely touching his mouth with her own, but the inexperience of the kiss had his blood heating.

Theo opened her mouth to his and was rewarded by the thrust of Jack's tongue. He took control of the kiss, and Theo helplessly responded to it. She couldn't help the soft sounds she made in the back of her throat as he thoroughly tasted her.

Jack felt her soften against him as she kissed him back. The tentative touch of her tongue encouraged him. She may not think he was attracted to her, but her response told him that she was attracted to him.

Jack pulled his mouth from hers, kissing a path down her neck to her collarbone. His hands went to the hem of her t-shirt. The skin at her waist was smooth. He knew because he had been changing the bandages on that soft skin. His hands ached to touch the even softer flesh above. He looked into Theo's eyes as he started to remove the shirt, and she gave in to him with no protest.

Theo couldn't believe she was standing here with Jack while he removed her clothing. She had imagined him touching her, but the reality of it was overwhelming. Jack's hands were large, the calluses on his fingertips rough on her skin. When he kissed the swell of her breasts over the cups of her bra, she grasped his hands in hers.

"Jack?" Theo pulled slightly away from him so the only thing touching was their hands.

"Yes, Theo?" Jack ached to pull her back to him, but her voice had trembled when she said his name.

"I'm not very experienced. We probably shouldn't do this."

Jack's body tightened at her words. He probably shouldn't be turned on by her inexperience, but he was. Some deep, primitive part of him wanted her all to himself. "Theo, that's not a good reason to stop. If you don't want me, then say so. If you do want me, we'll take this nice and slow."

Theo trembled. She did want Jack. She just didn't want to disappoint him. "I do want you, Jack."

Jack didn't respond with words. Instead, he set about seducing her so she would forget to be nervous, forget that it had been a long time for her. He didn't want thoughts of any other man in her mind; he wanted her focused totally on him.

Theo went lax in his arms as he began making love to her. He found parts of her body she hadn't known longed for his touch. He removed her bra and loved her breasts with his hands and mouth. Though not very large, he seemed fascinated by them. They hardened and swelled under his touch, and she eagerly lifted herself for more.

Jack once again picked up Theo, this time setting her on

the bed. He removed his shirt. He then discarded his jeans and socks but kept his briefs on for the moment. He then slid Theo's sweatpants down her legs, leaving her in only her panties. He then realized there was one thing he had forgotten.

Theo stayed completely still when Jack leaned over her and began pulling her hair from its knot. He gently unrolled it and smoothed it over her shoulders and down her chest. When he bent to kiss her, his hands fisted in the hair he had released. When he lifted his mouth from hers, there was satisfaction in his gaze. "You have no idea how beautiful you are, Theo."

Not willing to argue, Theo simply pulled Jack's mouth back to hers. She wanted more of his drugging kisses. When he kissed her, she forgot to be embarrassed or nervous. His mouth was like a drug, and she felt her senses swirl around her.

Jack explored Theo's body, turned on by her soft sighs and moans. When her hands found their way to his body, it was he who shuddered. When she tried to pull away, he would drag her hands back, showing her how and where he wanted to be touched. It wasn't long before he no longer had to encourage her. She made a foray over his body that had him fighting for control. And when her hands strayed inside his briefs, he was pretty sure his eyes crossed. He'd imagined her hands on him, her soft fingers gently touching and stroking him. She forgot her inexperience and explored him with greater purpose as her confidence grew.

Jack pulled away and removed his briefs. He also went to his bag and pulled out a condom. Back at his apartment, he had optimistically tucked a box into his bag. "Now it's my turn."

Theo barely heard him as she got her first good look at Jack completely naked. She had touched his body, but it hardly seemed real. His body was magnificent. At six-five, there was a lot of him. His shoulders were broad and his chest wide. The spattering of hair couldn't conceal the muscles beneath. His stomach was flat, and the hair tapered past his waistline. And when her gaze drifted lower, she couldn't help but be excited and just a little bit nervous at the same time. Jack was not a lightweight, and he wasn't in that part of his anatomy either. Even his thighs and calves were large and roped with muscle.

"I'm not sure if I should be flattered or cover up." Jack sat on the edge of the bed for a moment, rolling the condom on. When he finished, he turned back to Theo.

Theo swallowed the lump in her throat. "Probably both."

Jack laughed, but there wasn't any humor in it. He leaned over Theo, quickly tugging her panties off. He tossed them across the room. He eased himself over her, encouraging her to open her thighs to him with his hands. He traced the inside of those creamy thighs, enjoying the texture of her flesh. His other hand wrapped around her bottom, enjoying the soft curves.

"Have I told you that I admire you from behind?" Jack's hands further widened her thighs and slowly eased between them.

Theo felt Jack's hand caressing said behind, his fingers making a slow path between them to where her body was aching to be touched. She could feel herself dampening his fingers, but all she could think was that she needed more.

Jack kept his touch light at first, stroking and opening her body slowly to his. He could feel how tight she was, and he didn't want to hurt her. He had to be careful when choosing his bed partners. A man of his size couldn't seduce a small woman. But he knew just by looking at Theo that she was going to be perfect for him. He could feel her curves and hollows aligning with his body as he now lay fully between her legs. He hated that the condom kept him from feeling all the damp heat of her; he wanted nothing more than to strip it off and take her, flesh to flesh. But common sense kept him from doing so.

Theo lifted herself, wanting more of Jack's touch. His fingers were teasing her, slowly penetrating her body, pulling away, then gently returning. His touch was driving her mad. She couldn't believe how close she was to begging for his complete touch. Instead of begging, she wrapped her legs around him as tightly as she could, trying to make him finish what he had started.

Jack removed his hands, cupping her bottom, allowing her to bring him closer to the entrance of her body. He arched her hips, hoping to help ease the way. He entered her shallowly at first, only giving her a small part of what she craved. Slowly he increased his penetration, gently, but completely opening her to him when her fingernails dug into his back. When he finally seated himself fully inside her, it was he who moaned, and he who trembled.

Theo lost all sense of self as Jack made love to her. Her mind could only focus on the feel of Jack deep inside her body, focus only on the thick feel of him as his hips moved against hers. At first, he kept his thrusts slow, but they gained speed as they both strained to reach completion. Theo nearly wept as her body tightened around his; her need for him was so great. She barely heard her cries as her body convulsed around his, the power of her release beyond anything she had ever imagined.

The sound of Theo's soft scream sent Jack over the edge. He kissed her then, his shout of satisfaction muffled by the connection of their mouths. He didn't want the moment to end, so he thrust one last time against her, holding her to him as tightly as he dared.

Theo slowly came back to her senses, enjoying the feel of Jack lying heavily atop her. She hadn't realized how heavy he was while they were making love, but she was enjoying the feel of him half asleep on top of her, even though she could barely breathe.

"I should move." Jack started to ease off of Theo, but she clasped him to her.

"Not yet." Theo kissed his chest, trying to hold him to her.

Jack eased his body off to the side, keeping their bodies linked. She seemed to need this closeness, and he had to admit he did too.

Theo's thigh climbed his, happy now that she could still feel him on her, and in her, but could breathe again. Her body was tingling in the aftermath, also something she hadn't imagined.

"So, do you believe me now that I find you attractive?" Jack's tone was teasing, but it was a serious question, one he wanted an answer to.

Theo looked into his bright blue eyes. They had made love in the middle of the afternoon, so light poured into the bedroom. There was no hiding from him in the dark. She sighed and relaxed. "Yes, I guess I do. I guess I don't understand why, but I believe you."

"I'll take that for now." Jack kissed her and rolled onto his back, taking her with him. Theo was draped over his chest, looking as if she could fall asleep at any moment. When she did doze off, he slowly separated their bodies and put Theo under the covers.

He rose and went to the bathroom to wash up. When he came back, Theo was lying on her side, her hand where his head had been. He eased under the covers next to her, careful not to wake her. Given her doubts, he wanted to be next to her when she woke. Jack didn't sleep but held her and let his mind drift. Now that he had her, he wasn't going to let her go. She might not yet be in love with him, but her physical reactions to him told him that she could. It was enough for now.

Chapter Seven

Theo thought she might feel a bit awkward with Jack when she woke. Jack didn't give her the chance. When she stirred and woke, he was still with her. He kissed her, perhaps a bit more passionately than she had expected given how drained she still felt, but she had participated wholeheartedly. Jack was a great kisser. Now sitting back in the kitchen, wrapped only in Jack's robe instead of her own, she was completely relaxed.

"I still think I should consult your father. And I think John may be able to help." Jack took a sip of his coffee, his mind back on work.

"How so? What does John do?" Theo didn't know much about John, other than his being Jack's friend.

"He and Isabelle work for The Heart's Way Foundation. It's a charity that helps other charities. They met through a consulting job John had with a foundation Isabelle worked for. Turns out they knew each other when they were kids. Isabelle was having some trouble with her brother, who liked to pound on his girlfriends. John hired me to find him after her brother threatened her. Things got complicated after that. The owner of The Gables, the foundation Isabelle worked for, ended up being the one who funded her brother's illegal activities. And not one to pass up the opportunity, Isabelle's brother ended up attacking John in a warehouse rented by Isabelle's boss and vandalizing Isabelle's apartment. In the end, it all came down to her boss embezzling money and using her parolee brother to vandalize his property so he could collect insurance money. His goal was to make her brother look responsible and flee the country before anyone was the wiser. Both men ended up in jail."

That certainly explained why Isabelle understood how she was feeling. But his explanation didn't answer her question. "So how will that help you find a killer?"

"I got to thinking about Donovan's political aspirations. John knows a lot of different political movers and shakers in the city. He knows pretty much anyone who thinks they're someone. He might know some of the people Donovan was trying to recruit for his political campaigns, since he had his sights set on state politics, not local. This is Los Angeles, and I guarantee you that Donovan spent some time here. John might know more about the people Donovan was involved with than the papers."

Theo thought about that and realized Jack was right. It was time to call in recruits. "When are they returning?"

"This Thursday." Jack began compiling a list of names for John. He found the list of Donovan's campaign donors; unfortunately, it was not a short list.

"So soon?" Theo leaned back in her chair, curling her legs under her.

Jack glanced up at the dismayed sound of her voice. He couldn't help his grin. "Don't worry, I'll still sneak into your room."

Theo blushed at that. Ready or not, she had started a

relationship with Jack. She didn't know where it would end up, but she had high hopes. Jack said he had feelings for her. Perhaps those feelings could grow into something permanent. Lying in bed with Jack made her realize she had been lying to herself. She wasn't just lusting over Jack; she was in love with him. It hardly seemed possible, but she couldn't delude herself into thinking that what she felt was temporary.

"So, what are we going to do now? Wait for John?"

"No. I'm going to call your father. He pays more attention to politics than I do. Our firm has worked with a lot of different people in the city, and a lot of those people owe your father some favors. It's time he collects."

Theo sat while she listened to Jack on the phone. If she got the gist of the conversation, her father was on his way. "I take it he has the address."

"Yeah. John and the foundation have been clients of ours for years. The three of us have hung out a few times. It's easier to have a guys' night here than at my apartment. And no offense, but your dad's house is stuffy. And his housekeeper is extremely disapproving."

Theo rose. "I always called her the enforcer. Joanie keeps that house running smoothly and doesn't tolerate people making messes. My father is too afraid of her to fire her."

Jack laughed and rose too. "I suppose you'd better get dressed. Your father might think he wouldn't mind if we developed a relationship, but seeing you in nothing but my robe might be a bit more than he bargained for."

That gave Theo pause. "What about my dad not minding a relationship between us?"

Jack pulled her into his arms, kissing her between words. "Your father is not stupid. He could see the way I looked at you; the way I treated you. It didn't feel right making a move on the boss's daughter, but I'd recently decided that I had to have you. I was relieved when he said that to me. I wasn't sure how I was going to break it to him."

Theo heard most of what Jack said, but his kisses were distracting her, which she was sure was his intention. "I suppose getting involved with my father's employee isn't much better. Of course, now I'm involved with his business partner. Could make for complications."

"I don't see how. The only complication I was worried about was your father's reaction. And you don't expect to keep working for your father forever. Once this mess is sorted out, we won't have any issues keeping work and our relationship separate."

Theo closed her eyes. She realized how complicated this could get. She was job hunting, and that job hunting would take her away from Jack. Even if they proved Donovan was guilty, there was no guarantee she'd have better luck finding a job. And she hadn't told him yet that she had a job interview. She had just found out about it last night. It would take her hundreds of miles away from him.

Jack felt her body tense. Instead of releasing her, he deepened the kiss. He didn't know what she was thinking, but he wanted her thoughts solely on him. Her soft moan and the sudden grip of her hands in his hair told him he had succeeded. He backed her up against the table and lifted her onto it. His hands went inside her robe, caressing her bare flesh. "We have to stop. Your dad isn't that far away."

The mention of her father was enough to cool her off. She wasn't ready for her father to know about her and Jack. Jack held her steady as she slid off the table, and then she headed to her bedroom. She closed the door and leaned against it. She didn't know what to do. Should she thank the law firm and decline the interview? Should she go anyway and see what happened? Jack had just signed a contract that made him a full partner in her father's firm. Knowing Jack, he hadn't made that decision lightly. Theo couldn't ask him to give up the partnership for her. But she didn't see how she could stay. One thing she wasn't was a woman of leisure. She had worked since she turned sixteen. Even while she completed law school, she had worked.

But thinking of Jack, of being in love with Jack, and the things he had done to her body, she didn't know how she was going to give him up. Or if she even could. Idly Theo wondered if centerfold types had these types of problems. Certainly, she had never had them before and had never expected to.

Theo put on a pair of jeans instead of her sweatpants. Though the loose band of the sweatpants didn't rub the stitches on her back, she couldn't face her father in them. She was afraid she would keep remembering Jack sliding them off of her. She pulled a work blouse out of the closet as well, hoping a bit of professionalism would help her keep her composure. She glanced at the dresser for her hairpins and remembered they were in Jack's room. She snuck across the hall and gathered her clothes, blushing again when she found her underwear tossed across the room and her hairpins scattered on the bedside table. She snuck back to her room and quickly put her hair up in a twist.

She had just made herself presentable when she heard her father's voice. She took a deep breath and left the bedroom. "Hi, Dad."

Tom greeted her with a kiss on the cheek. "Heard Jack here could use some help. Been a while since I left the office and made sure I wasn't being followed. Sometimes I miss the old days."

Jack sat on the couch. "I prefer routine and ordinary."

"You always were a bit of a stick in the mud. For a guy who looks like he could take out a bear with his bare hands, you always were dull." Tom shot his daughter an amused grin and took a seat.

Feeling a bit like a third wheel, Theo took the loveseat. Despite their many differences, in some ways, her father and Jack were a lot alike. And when she saw them together, she couldn't help but notice how comfortable they were around each other. The light kiss on her cheek that her father gave her stunned her. He had never been given to displays of affection. If this were Tiffany's doing, then she could only applaud the woman's efforts at changing her father.

Jack frowned at Theo. She was sitting as far away as possible. "I want to know more about the men Donovan knew. I keep going back to the political angle. It's the only one that makes sense. We know he was into drugs, but it's not as if he were a petty dealer in a back alley. This was big time. And with his political aspirations, any rumor of involvement with drugs or drug cartels was bound to do some serious damage. He became CEO of a law firm with hardly any experience. He was making a huge salary and earning an impressive bonus. But even with that, getting into politics is expensive, and he needed backers. I've got a list of names. I'm going to run them by John when he returns but wanted your take."

Tom took the list from Jack. "Some of these men are heavy hitters, Jack. I can probably rule a few out. There is no way Holyfield and Stoker would be involved in anything illegal. They're two of the most respected businessmen in Los Angeles, and I know them personally. They would be more likely to lead the charge against a man like Donovan than join him."

Jack made notes on his laptop. "The others?"

"Mmm.   There are several names here I am not acquainted with. But one name is standing out. Colm O'Carroll. His father, Quinn, was an Irish immigrant. Quinn was a member of my club. Used to talk about how his son was always getting himself into trouble. His father bought him out of most of his troubles, but there was one occasion he got caught with illegal substances and an unregistered gun. It took every bit of finagling Quinn could manage to get his son a light sentence. Was out of jail in about six months. Didn't see too much of Quinn after that. Unfortunately, he died of a heart attack last year. He liked his Irish whiskey and cigars a bit too much."

"I didn't find a record of it. Wonder why?" Jack pulled up one of his search programs and did a further dive into Colm's history.

"As you said, his father had money. Wouldn't surprise me if he was able to hush the whole thing up. I've no doubt you'll find his criminal record on file, but I don't think it made the press. Quinn kept a low profile, so his son's arrest wouldn't have been big news."

"I wonder who his attorney was?" Theo tucked her legs under her and tried to think if she remembered any cases with O'Carroll as the client. Nothing came to mind, but she wasn't close to that part of the firm's business.

"That's a good question." Jack added additional search parameters.

Twenty minutes later, Jack had her answer. "Angelo Marino was the attorney assigned to the defense, according to court documents. When Quinn died, Colm would have inherited his father's estate. That puts a lot of money in his hands. It's possible Angelo introduced Colm to Donovan after he inherited."

"It's worth pursuing." Tom went further down the list. "Another name on this list I recognize is Randolph Turner. He wants to be a big player, but his reputation is a bit shady. Rumors are he likes hookers and isn't shy about paying top dollar. But that's just a rumor. Again, he rarely makes the papers, but he would do just about anything to get media attention. I'm not sure if he would care if it's good or bad press. He's got the money to play, but not too many people will let him into their social circles."

Jack did some brief digging. "So far, nothing else ties him to Donovan other than a large cash donation. It's possible he was just trying to buy his way into the boy's club. I doubt Donovan would have turned the money down, no matter where it came from. It's easy to suppress that type of information by turning people's attention to other larger donors. His lawyer is with a different firm. No ties to the

Marinos, but I'll keep digging."

"If I took a guess, I'd say the other names are just average citizens. I can run a check back at the office to see if any of them have ties to the Marinos. But John may know some of these names. I'll start the search tomorrow and email you the results. It might take a while." Tom rose, tucking the paper into his jacket pocket.

"So, onto more personal topics. When's the wedding, and when is the baby due?" Jack leaned back against the couch, pleased he had caught Tom off guard.

"Knew my daughter couldn't keep a secret. The baby is due in about four months. Tiffany waited to tell me until she couldn't hide it anymore. The wedding will be as soon as I can arrange it. Tiffany wants it at the house, and I have a judge friend willing to officiate it. We're keeping it close, family only. Tiffany's sister and her husband will be there. Tiffany's aunt something or other will be there as well. Then it will be you and Theo, my nephews, and my brother and his wife."

"Sounds good. Theo and I will come together."

Tom gave Jack a narrowed gaze, but nothing on Jack's face gave any indication that the relationship between him and his daughter had changed. "Good. And make sure she gets a new dress. I don't want to see that ugly black dress of hers."

Theo felt a little hurt by her father's words, but she didn't blame him. The dress she'd worn to John and Isabelle's wedding was the same one she'd worn to his last two birthday parties.

Jack saw Tom to the door. "I don't particularly care what

she wears."

Tom saw a betraying glimmer in Jack's eyes. He shut the door behind him and whistled on his way to the car. He had hoped Jack would finally make a move. Looked like he finally had.

Jack turned back to Theo. "At least we have someone else to dig into besides the Marinos. I'm interested in what John will have to add. But I do think you'll need a new dress."

Theo watched Jack as he dropped beside her on the loveseat. "You just said you don't care what I wear."

Jack took her hand in his. "I don't. But I think we'll be making an appearance at The Heart's Way Foundation Charity Ball, and the black dress won't do. The event is black tie all the way. There is usually an assortment of politicians and actors in attendance, and they dress to impress. John and Isabelle had to cut their honeymoon short because of it. The ball is on Saturday. It can't hurt to feel a few people out about the Marinos, and perhaps about Donovan. His murder made headlines, so it wouldn't be unusual for people to speculate about what happened. Donovan had an invitation to the ball; I checked."

Theo had never been to a charity ball before, and the words "politicians and actors" had her in a panic. "Jack, I don't know what to buy."

Jack saw a trickle of fear in her eyes. Only his Theo would be scared over a dress. "I'm sure Isabelle can help on short notice."

Using the grip he had on her hand, Jack pulled Theo onto his lap. His size had its advantages. "You'll be fine. Trust me."

Theo tipped her neck to the side while Jack placed biting kisses on her exposed skin. The skin stung ever so slightly, but he quickly soothed it with his tongue. His hands went to her blouse, and he slowly unbuttoned it, revealing her skin inch by inch. She trembled under his caresses, leaning back against him to give him better access. When his hands found her breasts, she practically purred.

Jack dug a condom out of his back pocket and set her on her feet. He quickly stripped both him and her.

Theo saw what he had in his hands. "Did you have that in your pocket while you were sitting there talking to my father?"

Jack cupped her bottom, lifting her and wrapping her legs around his waist. "Yes, I did. I grabbed it while you were getting dressed. I was half afraid the stupid thing would jump out of my pocket."

Theo giggled. "It certainly would have made a statement."

Jack backed her up against the wall, lifting her slightly so he could reach her breasts with his mouth. Her giggle turned to a moan, and he felt himself grow even harder against her. Theo writhed against him, trying to bring him closer to the entrance of her body. Knowing this time wasn't going to last long, he braced her against the wall and handed her the condom.

She looked at it, then Jack. She'd never put one on a man before but figured it couldn't be that difficult. She tore the wrapper and slowly rolled it on him. His breathing was even faster by the time she finished.

"I think next time I'll just wear the thing. I was so aroused while talking to your father; it would have stayed on."

That made Theo giggle even harder. When he carefully thrust into her, the giggles dissolved. Jack had her braced as he quickly thrust into her, over and over. Very quickly, she felt the now familiar tightening of her body, and her head fell on his shoulder. She bit Jack's shoulder, desperate now, her breath coming in pants.

Jack felt the bite of her teeth and reveled in it. His Theo could be quite feisty when he was inside her. When she practically screamed her release in his ear, he thrust one last time, taking himself completely to the hilt. She pulsed around him, and he gave in to his release.

This time, Jack kept his body pressed against her to keep her from falling. He brushed the loose tendrils of her hair that had come free. "Who knew sweet Theodora was a screamer?"

Theo was too spent to be embarrassed. "I've never screamed before. But then, no one has ever made me feel like this."

Jack eased himself from her, enjoying the clenching of her body as he did so. "I'm glad, Theodora. I don't want you to scream for anyone else but me."

Theo saw the darkening of his blue eyes, the familiar glimmer banked. This was not a time to tease. "There won't be anyone else but you, Jack."

Jack roughly kissed her and then dragged her with him to the bathroom. "We should have a shower, and then we should go out for dinner. If we don't go someplace public, I won't be able to keep my hands off you."

Theo didn't think that was such a bad thing, but the ache in her thighs and deep in her body told her he was right. She wasn't used to making love, and she was already feeling sore. They'd made love twice in less than six hours. She didn't know a whole lot about male anatomy but figured he could use a rest, too.

Theo quickly washed her hair and grabbed the conditioner. She watched Jack as he washed his hair. He then grabbed a washrag and lathered it up. He handed it to her and turned his back to her. Theo quickly washed Jack's back, but that wasn't quite enough. She wrapped her arms around him, rubbing the washrag over his chest from behind. When her hands went lower, she felt his renewed interest.

"My turn." Jack finished washing up, then hauled Theo under the spray. He rinsed the conditioner from her hair, then washed her body from head to toe. He lingered at her breasts, thighs, and buttocks.

Theo was trembling by the time Jack finished washing her and helped her out of the shower. She wrapped her hair in a towel and stood stock still while Jack ran a towel over her. Instead of handing her the towel, he dried himself off. Given his semi-state of arousal, she guessed he needed her to keep her hands to herself for now.

Jack sent her to her bedroom to get dressed and walked to his door. "Theo?"

She turned to face him.

"Keep your hair down."

She watched as he shut the door after his command. Smiling to herself, she did as she was told.

Jack took Theo to his favorite Italian restaurant. It was a nice, romantic place to take her for a first date, but still casual enough that neither of them had to change into something nicer.

They ordered their food, and Jack realized how quiet Theo was being. Jack took her hand across the table. "Regrets?"

Theo shook her head. "No. No regrets. It's hard to regret something you've wanted to do for a while."

"How long is a while?" Jack had to ask.

"Since I met you, probably. Or maybe the second time. You're an amazing man, Jack."

Jack was taken aback. "You're serious."

Theo just nodded her head.

Jack kissed her knuckles. "When I think of all the time we've wasted. I think I wanted you from the second time I met you, too. The first time I was interested. The second time I was intrigued. After that, you had my full attention."

Theo blushed; the kiss he placed on her hand was probably one of the sweetest gestures anyone had made to her. "You have my attention now."

Jack kept her hand in his but rested them on the table. "So, what were you thinking about?"

Theo let her gaze drift across the restaurant. "I have a request for a job interview."

Jack tensed. "Where?"

Theo's eyes met his, her turmoil plain to see. "Not here. If I get the job, I'll be leaving California."

"And after today..." Jack let the words trail off.

"I don't want to go. But there are no job prospects for me here."

Jack was touched. "And I don't want you to go. And I

can't go."

Theo nodded. "You just signed a partnership deal with my dad."

"I've worked hard to get where I am, Theo. I don't know if I can give it up."

Theo pulled her hand away. "And I wouldn't want you to. You have roots here that I don't have. My entire life is in upheaval. I suppose I could stay on with my dad, but it's not really what I want to do."

"I can't tell you what to do, Theodora. I can only tell you what I want. You have to decide on your own." Jack tucked his hands in his lap to keep from grabbing her and begging her to stay.

Theo dropped her head. She had never felt so confused or so adrift. Jack was a bright spot in what had been a difficult few months. She'd been fired, found a dead body, and was attacked. On the other hand, she was going to be a sister, her father was getting married again, and it seemed like a good idea this time, and she'd made mad, passionate love with Jack. Twice. And Jack wanted her to stay.

"Why don't you go to the interview. It may help you make your decision."

Theo realized he was not going to make this easy for her. And if their relationship fizzled, she had to have a plan. Everything had happened so fast.

Dinner was tense between them. Both of their thoughts were on the interview and what it would mean for their relationship should she leave.

When they got back to the house, Jack poured both of them a drink. They settled down on the couch. Jack tossed the drink back, and Theo sipped hers.

"Do you want to sleep alone?" Jack kept his gaze on the empty glass.

"No." Theo's voice was quiet but sure. "I'm sorry, Jack. I just don't know what to do."

Jack let out a deep sigh. "What I do know is that you don't have to make that decision right now."

Theo scooted next to Jack and rested her head on his shoulder. She relaxed when his arm came around her, hugging her to his side. They stayed that way until it was time for bed.

Chapter Eight

"It is so good to be home." Isabelle tossed her bags in the entryway while John brought in their luggage.

John kicked the door closed behind him. "I'll second that."

Jack greeted the returning couple at the door while Theo hung back. "Welcome back."

"We came back with more stuff than we left with. Now we have to figure out where to put it all." John teased Isabelle.

Isabelle kissed her husband. "Don't worry, some of these tacky souvenirs are for Jack and Theo."

Jack kissed Isabelle's cheek. "Just what I always wanted."

Isabelle chuckled and threw herself down on the sofa. "I think we'll sleep for a week."

John sat next to her and patted her knee. "No rest for the weary. You've got a party to check on."

"I left very capable people in charge." Isabelle looked at Jack. "Are you coming?"

Jack took a seat next to Theo and took her hand, clearly broadcasting the change in their relationship. "As a matter of fact, I am. I need to talk to John about something, and you need to help Theo find a dress."

Isabelle looked at a guilty-looking Theo. Isabelle wasn't sure what the guilty look was for, but she was very pleased to see Jack staking a claim. "I'd love to. Give me the night to recuperate, and we can hit my favorite store in the morning."

"I appreciate the help. I have no idea what to buy for a charity ball." Theo said, leaning slightly against Jack.

"I'm constantly attending some fundraiser or another. If you were my size, I'd lend you something of mine, but you've got a few inches on me." Isabelle closed her eyes and rested her head on the back of the couch.

Jack sat back and asked, "So, how was Hawaii?"

Isabelle's head perked right back up as she went into enthusiastic detail about her honeymoon. The four of them kept the conversation going through dinner until bedtime.

"I don't know about the rest of you, but I'm exhausted." John rose, pulling his wife with him. The heat in his gaze was not that of a tired man.

Isabelle went with him without hesitation. "I look forward to our shopping trip in the morning, Theo. Night, Jack."

Jack and Theo watched the pair head to their bedroom; Isabelle's giggles could be heard clearly before the door shut.

Jack turned the lights off while Theo headed to her room. He saw Theo glance over at him, a question in her eyes, and he simply turned the alarm on and followed her to her room.

Theo sat on the edge of the bed while she waited for Jack. He came into the room and closed the door. Her room was farthest from the newlyweds' bedroom, not that they were worried about the couple down the hall.

Jack stripped his shirt over his head and quickly removed his jeans. Wearing just his boxers, he crossed to Theo. She lifted her arms when he grabbed the hem of her shirt so he could easily remove it. His fingers went to the snap of her jeans, while Theo unhooked her bra. He stripped her jeans and underwear off, leaving her nude before him.

"You make me ache, Theo." Jack dropped his boxers, then scooted Theo back onto the bed, covering her body with his own.

"You do the same to me." Theo whispered the words back to Jack. Pressed up against her the way he was, she knew his body was fully aroused. She wanted him inside her now. She grabbed the condom she'd left on the nightstand earlier that day and handed it to him.

Jack rolled it on and didn't need any further urging. He kissed her deeply and very slowly penetrated her body. She wasn't completely ready for him, but she kept a grip on his back, not letting him ease away.

Theo's thighs climbed his legs, the deep, throbbing ache inside demanding immediate relief. Jack pulled back and surged back into her. She felt herself melt around him.

Jack quickly established the rhythm, bringing Theo to satisfaction. He covered her mouth with his so that the couple down the hall wouldn't hear Theo's scream.

Theo lay still, Jack still hard inside her. Her brown eyes held his. "What's wrong?"

Jack just smiled and kissed her again. "Nothing. I just want to make you scream again."

Theo smiled and held on. A short time later, for the second time, Theo loudly voiced her release in Jack's mouth. This time he went with her.

* * *

"This one would look terrific on you." Isabelle handed a deep plum gown with silver embellishments to Theo.

Theo looked at the dress, torn between wanting to let Isabelle help her and distressed because there was no way she was going to pull this off. She wasn't the type to wear fancy dresses, certainly not ones with sparkles on them. Her gaze drifted to the rack of more demure dresses, but Isabelle had already vetoed every dress Theo had suggested.

"So, what happened between you and Jack? It's obvious the two of you are involved." Isabelle continued combing the racks. The saleswoman had backed off when she saw her favorite client. Isabelle always did her own shopping.

"We sort of ended up in bed together after an argument. I couldn't believe Jack was interested in me. He told me he was, but I didn't believe him. He set out to prove me wrong."

Isabelle's gaze softened as she listened. "I seduced John. But he was willing. He wasn't sure a relationship between us was a good idea. His body kept telling me otherwise every time he kissed me. But he would stop and pull back. He said there was no going back to the way things were if we went to bed together. Boy, was I glad he meant it. I was hopelessly in love with him."

"I'm in love with Jack." Theo heard herself blurt it out.

Isabelle gave her a huge grin. "I'm so happy for you two. Jack is great. He used to flirt outrageously with me just to annoy John. And if I hadn't already been in love with John, Jack would have been a great catch. What woman wouldn't want Jack? Tall, dark, and handsome. Plus, he has those amazing, bright blue eyes. A girl could lose herself in them."

It was odd to hear the woman speaking so frankly about what could have been between her and Jack. But seeing the two of them together, and the fact that John didn't seem worried, she knew nothing did or ever would develop between them.

"I know what you mean. I've had a crush on Jack since we met a few years ago. I'm Tom Landry's daughter."

Isabelle's head shot up in surprise. "Really? It's hard to imagine him with a daughter. Tom Cat, that's how I think of him. Always with a new lady."

Theo thought that was an apt description of her father. Or it was. "Actually he's settling down. I found out he's getting married, and his fiancée is pregnant."

"Wow." Isabelle handed Theo another dress, this one red with a plunging neckline. "That must be weird, your dad having a baby. Of course, it's probably weirder for him, what with a daughter in her twenties."

"Thirties. I'll be thirty before the baby is born." Theo looked at the red dress. The drapery on it was beautiful but would leave her way too exposed. "After I find a dress for the charity ball, I have to find something for his wedding. Maybe I'll come back here."

Isabelle kept going through the racks. "This place has just about everything you need for any occasion. A friend of mine owns the store, so I rarely go anywhere else."

Theo looked around. The clothes were beautiful, but nothing like what she was used to wearing. For the first time, excitement stirred in her belly. She wanted to look beautiful for Jack.

The two women spent the next couple of hours trying on

and discarding dresses. After the perfect dress was chosen, Isabelle grabbed a few accessories to add to the look when Theo admitted she didn't have any jewelry to wear.

Theo had just finished paying for the dress, shoes, and accessories when she spied a knee-length sheath of silvery gray. She stepped away from the clerk to inspect the dress. It wasn't the sexy red dress she had imagined wearing for Jack, but the dress was stunning. The scooped neckline looked almost like a collar; the bodice was discreetly embellished with silver beading. The dress would reach her knees and would hug her slender curves.

Isabelle saw where Theo's glance had gone, and she took the garment bag from the cashier. "Now that would look beautiful on you at your father's wedding."

Theo glanced at Isabelle. "Do you mind?"

Isabelle smiled. "Not at all."

Theo grabbed the dress in her size and went to the dressing room. Though the dress covered most of her chest, her bare arms and the low back made her feel exposed. But the dress made her feel sexy. It fit like a glove, hugging and accentuating her figure. The silver shoes she had just purchased to go with her new gown would go with this dress, too. Without glancing at the price tag, she slipped out of the dress and hung it back up. There was no way she was leaving without it.

Isabelle helped carry Theo's purchases out. "Are you hungry? My treat."

Theo slid into the passenger seat of the sporty car. "I won't turn that down, not with what I just spent. I think I might have to dip into my savings to cover the cost."

Isabelle sent a worried glance at Theo. "I didn't mean to take you there if you couldn't afford it."

"It's okay. The dresses are beautiful. And I couldn't have done this without you. I'm sure you've noticed, but I'm not very good with fashion."

Isabelle hadn't wanted to say anything, but so far what she'd seen of Theo's wardrobe made the woman in her cringe. Her jeans were baggy and didn't quite fit right. The blouse was not a flattering color at all. And that black dress she had worn to her wedding was hideous. "It's just a matter of picking the right size, color, and shape. Once you know what looks good on you, you simply buy similar styles. I'm too busty to wear the silver dress you picked out, but you're slender and tall enough to pull it off. You'll look like a model in that dress. I'd look like I tried to stuff myself into someone else's clothes."

A model wasn't quite a centerfold, but Theo would take it. "Maybe I should take you shopping with me more often."

Isabelle turned out of the parking lot onto the main road. "If you stick with Jack, we'll be fast friends. John and Jack spend a lot of time hanging out."

They pulled into the parking lot of a popular sandwich shop. The two women ordered and took a seat.

"How serious do you think it is between you and Jack?" Isabelle asked the question she had been dying to ask since Theo told her that she was in love with Jack.

"I'm not sure. Jack said he wasn't looking for a fling. But I might leave." Theo bit her lip and looked at Isabelle.

"Leave?"

Theo thanked the waitress who dropped their food off

and left. "How much do you know about what's going on?"

"Not a lot. I just know that Jack is protecting you."

"A few months back, I found out the CEO of the law firm I worked for was smuggling drugs. I told the law partners, who said they didn't believe me. They smeared my name in the press after firing me. I went to work for my dad because no law firm would hire me. They believed all the lies my previous bosses spread about me. Then a few weeks ago, I found the CEO dead in his office. My dad and Jack were worried. Turns out they were right. A week ago, I was attacked and threatened. Jack's going to talk to John about some of the people on his list of possible suspects. And he plans on trying to fish for information at your charity ball."

Isabelle snorted at that. "Trust Jack to finally agree to come to one of my galas because he wants to grill the guests. I suppose I should be grateful regardless. And I'm so sorry for what you're going through. I've been there myself. But in my case, I knew who was trying to hurt me. My brother wanted revenge for helping put him in jail. Jack found him and led the cops to him."

Theo smiled at that. "Sounds like Jack. He's frustrated because he hasn't made much headway with my case. But neither have the police."

"I trust Jack will find him." Isabelle took a large bite of her sandwich. "But what about you and Jack? Will you leave?"

Theo picked up her sandwich but didn't take a bite. "I don't know. Things have been a bit tense between me and Jack since I told him about the job interview. He said I should go."

Isabelle frowned. "That doesn't sound like Jack. He's usually one to go after what he wants."

Theo digested that tidbit about Jack. Isabelle was right. Jack wasn't one to give up. "Maybe he doesn't want me as much as he thinks he does."

"Oh, Theo. I didn't mean it that way. Maybe Jack is scared of the decision you'll make. He has just as much invested in this relationship as you do. I can tell Jack cares about you. It's on his face every time he looks at you."

Theo wasn't sure about that. "If he asked me to, I would stay. But he said he won't do that. He said I know what he wants, that he doesn't want me to go, but he won't make the decision for me."

Isabelle patted Theo's hand. "In some ways, he's right. You have to make that decision. On the other hand, a woman wants to know she's wanted. Tell him to ask you to stay."

Theo shook her head. "I won't put him in that spot. Maybe I will go to the interview. It can't hurt. And after this is all over, Jack may not want me anymore. I'm not exactly his type."

Both women were silent for a few moments. There was truth in that statement. Isabelle felt bad for Theo. And for Jack. But the path to love wasn't always a smooth one, and it was a path each person had to walk on their own.

* * *

Theo wasn't sure what she expected for her first gala charity ball, but she was enjoying herself. She had come out of the bedroom earlier that evening feeling like Cinderella. She and Isabelle had decided on the plum-colored floor-length gown with silver embellishments. Theo had still been unsure, but with one look at Jack's stunned expression, she knew it was well worth it. For the first time since she told him about the job interview, he had kissed her without a hint of restraint. He'd smoothed his hands down her body, tracing the lines of the dress as it fell over her breasts and hips. In her heels, she was almost eye level with him. She had seen banked lust in his eyes, and it triggered a quick response deep in her body.

She wore silver earrings that were two-inch columns that sparkled a bit when the light hit them. She had once again pinned up her hair, but Isabelle had helped her style it with loose tendrils and a fall of curls down her back. Jack had fingered the tendrils, stroked the exposed nape of her neck, and then quickly ushered her out the door.

Jack came back to where Theo waited, his arm casually slipping around her waist. "So far, people are gossiping about Donovan's murder, but no one has any insight into who or why."

Theo glanced around the crowd. "From the looks of it, these people are not the type to find themselves involved in drugs and murder."

"No, they're not. But I had hoped." Jack kept his arm around Theo as they made rounds around the room. He nodded at John when they passed nearby. John was also keeping his ears open. Jack had given John the list, and he agreed with Tom. There were names they could eliminate, and there were a few that could be good for it. But he didn't know all the names either.

Jack was having a hard time concentrating on his job when Theo was looking incredibly sexy by his side. Isabelle had outdone herself. Theo's hair was up but framed her face. The makeup was subtle but deepened the brown of her eyes. And that dress hugged her body beautifully. With little effort, his Theo was stunning. He had to send more than a few warning looks to the men whose gazes lingered too long.

Jack was about to give up circling the room when he heard a low, sexy female voice behind him.

"Hi, Jack. I heard you've been asking questions about Colm O'Carroll." A petite blonde came up behind Jack and Theo.

"Well, I'll be. Selena. It's been a while. I thought you were away on business." Jack embraced the petite woman and kissed her cheek.

"I was, but I decided to return a bit early." Selena glanced over at the woman next to Jack and introduced herself before Jack could. "Hi, I'm Selena, an old client of Jack's."

Theo shook the hand held out. She couldn't help giving the woman a once over. Her slender form was draped in an exquisite white sheath. It highlighted the slightly tanned skin and slenderness of her form. And she couldn't help but notice her strawberry-blonde hair leaned a bit toward red tones. "I'm Theo. Nice to meet you."

"What exactly have you heard?" Jack led both ladies out to the terrace, to not be overheard. Selena was more than a client. She had helped him on a few cases and still did on occasion. There wasn't much that went on in the city she didn't know about. Also, she was one of the few women Jack considered a friend.

"I'm not sure I ever told you, but Colm O'Carroll was a cousin by marriage of my late husband. Once upon a time, Colm was always hanging around the office, trying to drum up work. He still occasionally pops through my door, mostly looking for handouts, though I've never given him one."

"I didn't realize. I don't want to drag up painful memories." Jack couldn't see the woman's eyes in the faint light, but he didn't want to bring up her husband's name unless he had to.

"Don't worry about it, Jack." Selena turned to Theo. "Jack investigated my husband for me shortly before his death. He also did some discreet digging into my husband's girlfriends."

"Girlfriends?" Theo asked, then flushed. "I'm sorry; that was rude."

Selena gave her a friendly smile. "Don't worry about it. I don't think there was a single person in town back then who didn't know about his affairs. He had so many, I lost count after a while. But he's been gone for six years. Most people are polite enough not to bring up his name, at least not in my presence."

Jack redirected the conversation. "What do you know about Colm?"

"It's not common knowledge, but he has managed to squander almost all of the funds he inherited from his father's passing within the last year. I know because he came crawling to me, this time desperate for quick cash. Said he had some items he wanted me to sell for him. I told him to get out. He became belligerent and I had to have Wallace toss him out. Then a few weeks ago, he came into some serious cash. Came into my office, waving the fact in my face that he doesn't need my money. I had my sources do some digging, and Colm is telling everyone he won it in a card game, but no one is claiming to be the one who lost to him. Tonight, I heard you were investigating Brandon Donovan's murder for a client, and then I heard Colm's name pop up. It's not hard to put two and two together."

Jack filled in the gaps. "Colm was one of the men who donated to Donovan's political campaign. And Colm's defense attorney on record is Angelo Marino. That ties Colm to both men."

Selena looked at Theo. "You're the woman the Marinos have been trashing in the press?"

"Yes, I am." Theo tucked her arm through Jack's. "We know Donovan was heavily into the drug trade. And I'm the one who found Donovan's body, though that is not public knowledge. We've been trying to come up with a reason, any reason, someone would have lured me there to find his body. Or why someone would now want me hurt."

Jack squeezed Theo to his side. "Someone attacked Theo while she was out getting lunch. I want the bastard who did it."

Selena glanced behind her and walked them deeper into the darkness outside the hotel. "Colm didn't use to be such a bad kid. Then he discovered cocaine. I don't know if that is still his drug of choice, but he hasn't stopped using. He was already dealing before he went to jail, though his father was in denial and tried to get him off. I imagine prison simply honed some of his less-than-desirable job skills. I wouldn't put it past him to be a thug for hire. And I can tell you that not all of the Marinos are as squeaky clean as they appear. And if they think Colm owes them for defending him and getting him a lighter sentence, it's probably not a stretch that one of the family members would use him for hired muscle."

Theo's mouth dropped open. "How do you know so much about the Marinos? Jack and I couldn't find even a hint of trouble in their pasts."

Selena waved a hand at that. "I run an antiquities business. I know a lot of people, people with a lot of money. Goods from all over the world flow through my warehouses. Angelo Marino has a weakness for Chinese antiques. He also is not discerning about where they come from. And he's not above using coercion or threats to get what he wants. At one time, he thought he could use my firm to bring in some, shall I say, suspect goods through my doors. I turned him down flat. He tried to blackmail me with threats that he would go to the police and accuse me of having murdered my husband."

Jack held up a hand to halt her. "Why am I just hearing about this?"

Selena just shrugged. "What's there to tell? My husband's death is old news. We both know nothing would come of his threats. I told him to go take a hike. I also had Wallace pay him a personal visit after hours. Let's just say he agreed to let bygones be bygones. I heard he went to a different firm to get his imports."

Something in Selena's tone grabbed Jack's immediate attention. "What firm?"

"It's called NSWE Trading Company. Want to take a

guess at who owns it?"

"I'll bite. Who?" Jack waited for her answer.

"O'Carroll. He inherited it from his father. It was one of several holdings his father had. It would be easy to use the company as a cover for the illegal drug trade. I regularly have federal agent types coming through my doors, inspecting my business to make sure nothing illegal is going on. With enough care and planning, it wouldn't be impossible to hide illegal dealings from the authorities."

"You're a scary woman, Selena. Can you send me what you've got on file?"

"Anything for you, Jack. I owe you."

Jack shook his head. "You don't owe me. And if you did, you've more than paid me back."

Selena kissed Jack's cheek and took one last look at Theo. "I wish you luck with this one. He's worth his weight in gold."

Jack and Theo watched Selena disappear into the crowd back inside the hotel.

"Who is she really?" Theo couldn't help but notice a fine tension in Selena as she talked to Jack.

"Selena really is an old friend. She had been married to her husband for only a few short weeks when she hired me to follow him."

"Because he was cheating?" Theo glanced back inside for a glimpse of the woman.

"No, because he tried to kill her."

"What?" Shock was clear in her voice.

"Selena didn't care that he was cheating on her. She knew he was when she married him. The marriage wasn't what anyone would call a love match. Her husband, Carter McGrath, owned an exclusive courier service. Carter and Selena's father wanted to go into a partnership, merging their two businesses. Carter's people would protect the goods coming and going through the company's doors. The marriage was a business move."

"Poor Selena. Why did she go through with the marriage?"

Jack shrugged. "All she says is that she had her reasons. She won't say what they were. But she had a few 'accidents' and started to become suspicious. Selena owned half the company. When her mother passed, the shares went to her. Her parents were divorced but were still business partners. With half ownership, Selena started taking a real interest in the business. Her father wasn't happy, but he couldn't stop her. I think he saw Carter as a way to control his daughter. Anyway, it turned out that her father and Carter were conspiring to have her killed. When his daughter died with no heirs, Carter would inherit her shares."

"And unite the two companies." Theo felt sudden pity for Selena. The woman didn't look any older than she was. She was a small, petite woman, and probably no match against two men set on murder.

"I found enough evidence to convict her father. He's in prison. But I couldn't find concrete evidence against her husband. He didn't deny the allegations, but he didn't incriminate himself either. Then her husband was killed in a plane crash. Selena was the number one suspect, but there was no proof. And I can say with conviction she had nothing to do with it. She was arrested and later released.

Thankfully I was able to keep it all covered up. No one knows she was accused, though of course, his death was no secret. People believe it was accidental, which was the authorities' final ruling. Rumors of murder or allegations against her would have ruined her reputation. I discreetly dug into the case and found enough evidence pointing away from her."

"Wow. That's quite a story. Were you two ever involved?" Theo glanced up at Jack.

Jack leaned down and kissed her, his lips lingering on hers. "No. Let's just say, though I like her, we aren't compatible."

Theo let it go. If Jack said they were never involved, then she believed him. "She's really pretty and seems like a tough cookie. You should have gone for it."

Jack laughed. "She was not only married when I met her, but she was also a client. Still is on occasion. She is also a consultant from time to time, though that's between you and me. When we met, there was no way she would have been ready for a serious relationship, though I will admit it crossed both of our minds at one point, and we kissed a few times. And though she acts tough, she's got a soft core."

"Why is she here tonight?" Theo held Jack's arm as he led her back inside.

"She's here tonight because she's one of the foundation's largest donors. I introduced her to John a few years ago. She liked John's sales pitch and got on board with the foundation."

Theo thought about the amount of money the people attending this gala, including Jack, had to shell out for a ticket. If she were one of the biggest donors, then her antiquities business must be doing exceptionally well.

"But she is exactly what I was hoping to find. Selena keeps her eyes and ears open. She's a fount of information. You see that tall man in the dark suit standing by the exit?"

Theo nodded. "Yes. He's been watching the room. I figured he was security."

"He's Selena's bodyguard. That's the Wallace she mentioned. First name is Ellis. I handpicked him for her. No one in this room gets within a few feet of her without her permission. He also happens to be an excellent hacker. He intimidates anyone who goes near her and gets her whatever information she wants."

Theo shivered. It sounded like a harsh way to live, always having to have someone looking over your shoulder. "She seemed to know an awful lot about the Marinos and Colm."

"She also gave me a great lead. First thing tomorrow I'll start digging into the NSWE Trading Company. Selena is right. It's the perfect cover for an illegal drug ring."

Chapter Nine

As soon as they got back to the house, Jack opened his email. The file Selena sent to him was a huge help. Included in the file was Colm's juvenile record. It was supposed to be sealed, but Jack wasn't going to complain. It wasn't legal for him to hack the court's servers, but it wasn't illegal for him to view it if someone happened to pass it along anonymously. The encrypted file, if someone tried to trace it, would have come from an overseas account with no owner. Jack wasn't a computer expert, but he knew Selena's bodyguard was. Selena wasn't too bad herself.

It seemed he had been looking in the right direction, just not the right players. Angelo Marino had a weakness for antiquities he shouldn't have in his possession. The type of antiquities that cost a small fortune. His bank records showed very large sums of money going out of his account into those of NSWE's. It looked like Ellis hadn't determined how Angelo might be involved in drugs, but it probably wasn't a stretch from black market antiquities to drugs. It might be time for a stakeout. Colm wasn't in hiding; quite the opposite. Following his activities was easier than following the Marinos. And it was possible Colm would meet with one of them.

A phone call to the office got one of his agents on Colm's trail. A second phone call got one on Angelo Marino. As an afterthought, he made a third call and put a tail on both Marlon and Angelo Junior. It was possible Angelo's sons were involved, too. He trusted his agents to be discreet and not be seen. He wanted to tail Colm himself, but if he knew Theo, she would insist on coming with him. As it was, she was waiting for him to come to her room. He wanted to see what Theo was wearing under that dress.

When he entered Theo's room, she was lying on the covers wearing nothing but a sexy white lace bra and panties. His body leapt to immediate attention.

Theo gave him what she hoped was a sultry smile. "I was wondering if you were going to make an appearance tonight."

Jack tugged the bow tie from his tuxedo and tossed it on the chair that sat near the dresser. "I wanted to see what Selena sent. But nothing was going to keep me from coming in here tonight."

Theo watched Jack undress. She had seen him in formal clothes at John and Isabelle's wedding, but she didn't think she'd ever get used to it. His tuxedo was not rented. It fit him to perfection. The white shirt didn't have any frills on it, but that didn't surprise her. Nothing about him hinted at any softness, not in his dress or in his manner.

"I know I said this earlier tonight, but I'll say it again. You looked incredibly beautiful tonight. And you look even better lying there, waiting for me."

Theo had debated whether to remain in the dress or not. It was easier when she undressed in front of him in the heat of the moment than it had been waiting for him in her new underwear. But the surprise and then the heat in his eyes when he set eyes on her had banished what remained of her uneasiness at being so exposed.

Jack sat on the bed, his fingers going to the edges of the lacy bra. He stroked her nipple under the fabric, enjoying the way Theo arched herself into his touch. Though they'd been lovers for only a few days, he was sure he'd never get enough of her reactions to his touch. He leaned down, nuzzling the fabric to the side, pulling her nipple fully into his mouth. Theo reached under her back to unhook the bra so Jack could pull it away. His hand went to the other breast, giving it the same attention. He paused only long enough to pull away the matching lace panties.

Theo's legs parted at the touch of his fingers on her thighs, and she was startled when Jack pulled her on top of him, then rolled so he was lying under her. Her thighs gripped his, her body tightening in anticipation of what was to come.

Theo had never made love this way, but she figured out quickly what to do. She lifted herself so she could take him inside her body. She slowly sank onto him, her body adjusting with slight pulsations as he stretched her. She moved slowly at first, gaining confidence and momentum as she went.

Jack lifted his hips so that he could sink further inside of her. The wet, sleek feel of her around him was enough to drive him mad. Then sanity asserted itself. Jack swore and stilled Theo.

Theo looked down at him in confusion, her breath coming in pants. She tried to move, but his hands held her. Jack was rock hard inside her, so she knew he wanted this.

"What?"

Jack gritted his teeth, trying not to lose control. "We forgot an important part of tonight's activities."

Theo stared in confusion for a moment, then realized he wasn't wearing a condom. Though it was probably not the right response, her body clenched tighter on his, and she desperately wanted to move.

Jack looked into her eyes, but she looked like she had no plans to budge. Swearing under his breath, he started to pull out of her. She moaned and tightened her thighs around him. "Theo?"

"Stay with me, Jack." Theo's words were barely audible, but the message was clear.

Jack knew it was madness, knew they were taking a risk, but he didn't want to leave her tight body. He pulled her back down onto him, grinding her against him. Her body reacted immediately. Theo's back arched and her body clenched tighter around his. For the first time since he'd first taken her, she didn't have the breath to make a sound. He lost all control, his hands moving Theo's hips in the rhythm he had halted. He felt himself pour into her, but the significance of it was lost in the pleasure of the moment.

Completely spent, Theo collapsed on Jack's chest. She could feel the sweat that had gathered between her breasts mingling with the perspiration on Jack's chest. Her thighs felt like rubber.

Jack swept his hands up and down Theo's back, waiting to see if guilt would eat at him for taking her without protection. But the feeling never came. Instead of releasing her, he pulled her mouth to his, burying his tongue in the dark recesses. His body slowly hardened inside her, while hers softened around him. He rolled them over and began thrusting inside her once again. Though slower, the experience was no less intense the second time around. Afterward, they fell into a deep sleep, their bodies pressed together and their limbs tangled.

* * *

"You look like the cat that swallowed the canary." Isabelle relaxed in the deck chair, Theo relaxing in the one beside her. The men were inside poring over names.

Theo blushed. When she woke this morning, Jack had already left. She was glad he was gone because she wasn't sure she could face him after what they had done. She could be pregnant right now, and she should be panicked. Instead, she felt content and relaxed. A baby would certainly make her decision about leaving easier, though it would complicate their newly formed relationship.

"Well?" Isabelle pressed. "I'd say I don't want to pry, but that would be a big fat lie. Though I probably have the same look on my face."

Theo had never had a girlfriend to confide in before. She wasn't ready to discuss her sex life with Jack in great detail with Isabelle, but she also was bursting to talk to someone. "Jack makes me happy. Probably as happy as John makes you."

"If he has anything in common with John, then I'd say he makes you very happy. Before John, I didn't know that making love could be so wonderful."

All Theo could do was nod. "I'd say they have a lot in common."

Isabelle giggled. "It's been quite the ride, and it doesn't get boring. John and I have our ups and downs, but he's the most reliable man I've ever met. Dependable. Jack is like that. Mature. Knows what he wants."

"You sound like Jack. The first time Jack made love to me, he told me he was old enough to know what he wants."

"What about you? Figured it out yet?"

Theo did know what she wanted, but without Jack asking her to stay, she had decided to go to the interview. Long-distance relationships weren't impossible if both people were committed. And with some distance, she might find out if what they had was something that would last or something that would fall apart. Just thinking about it made her chest ache.

Theo gazed up at the clouds above them. "I booked a flight. Jack is going to drive me to LAX tomorrow. I think part of him just wants me out of town for a few days, and this gets him what he wants. On the other hand, he's been very tense about it, too. He won't talk about it other than to say I need to do what's best for me."

Isabelle was quiet for a moment, sensing Theo's mood. Then she popped up. "Since you're going, let's go dig through your clothes, and we can pick out what you'll wear for your interview."

Theo let Isabelle distract her with clothes for the next half an hour. Isabelle chose a blouse and skirt, a pairing she wouldn't have chosen for herself, and grabbed her black pumps, telling her no stockings, and set her new silver earrings out. She then poked through Theo's cosmetic bag, adding a few items from her own bag for her to use.

By the time they were done packing her suitcase, stuffing it with what Isabelle determined would be her best clothing options, Theo had her emotions back under control. The pair then went to join the men. Jack and John were at the kitchen table going over the files Tom had sent over of what he had been able to dig up on Donovan's other campaign donors.

"So, what's the verdict?" Theo stood behind Jack, her hands on his shoulders.

"Colm is up to his eyeballs in trouble. He might just be desperate enough to do something drastic." Jack opened a web page and pinged Selena.

Theo saw Selena's image appear on the screen. The woman was once again dressed in white, a strand of perfectly shaped pearls around her neck. Diamonds glittered at her ears.

"What can I do for you?" Selena leaned back in an oversized chair. The artwork on the wall behind her was the real deal.

John came and stood beside Theo so Selena could see all three of them. "We have some questions for you about Colm. He's your nephew?"

Selena waved a hand to whoever was in the room and waited until they left. "Not exactly. He was a cousin through marriage of my husband. No blood relationship between them. Quinn O'Carroll had a brother who married my husband's aunt. Colm was the brother's wife's son from a previous marriage. He idolized my husband; he hung around a lot. O'Carroll even worked for my husband for a while until he went to prison."

Jack pulled up and shared a photo. "This is the most recent photo I could find of Colm. Does he still look like this?"

Selena nodded. "About. His hair is longer these days. Brushes his shoulders. I'd say he's just under six feet. And that photo doesn't show it, but he works out a lot. He's scary strong."

"Strong enough to subdue a woman Theo's size?" Jack asked.

"Definitely. As I said, he honed a few of his less desirable job skills in prison. He came out a lot bigger than he went in. He'd probably be bigger if he laid off the drugs. Unless he's using steroids, which I suppose is possible, too." Selena glanced at another computer screen.

"What else have you learned about NSWE?" Jack tapped a few keys and pulled up what he had found.

Selena leaned forward, her gaze serious. "You know me too well. NSWE was investigated while Quinn was still alive for selling stolen artifacts. Paid a huge fine, but the government couldn't prove he knew they were stolen. The company took a big hit. However, it was only one of several holdings Quinn had, so it didn't hurt his business portfolio. He paid the fines and made the appropriate apologies. Since then, the business has been clean. Or it was until Quinn died. We know Colm is working with Angelo Marino Senior on some shady antiquity deals, but as of yet the Feds haven't taken notice."

"What do you think the chances are that Quinn was

covering up a deal his son made?" John piped in while reading over Jack's shoulder.

"I'd say it's quite possible. As you both know, Quinn bailed Colm out of a lot of trouble. Kept hoping his son would straighten up. As far as I can tell, Quinn wasn't into anything illegal. Quinn had some questionable ethics, but he operated on the right side of the law. Colm was released from prison about a month before his father's heart attack. Though ruled a natural death, part of me wonders." Selena brushed a loose tendril of her hair, her mind totally focused.

Jack nodded. "There are certainly ways he could have accomplished his father's murder and mimicked natural causes."

Theo's hands tighten on Jack's shoulders. "I think I know him."

Jack, John, and Selena all focused on Theo. Jack was the one who spoke. "How?"

"I probably saw him around the law firm when Angelo was defending him. I can't remember."

"Do you think he could be the one who attacked you?" John took a seat.

"Maybe. If his hair is grown out, it's the right color. Selena said he was strong, and he is probably the right height and build to be my attacker."

Selena sent a file. "This picture is from my security cameras. It's only a couple of weeks old or so. It will be more recent than the image you have."

"Thanks, Selena. Anything else on the company?" Jack saved the image file.

"Not much. I've been digging around, and nothing is

coming up as a red flag. I will add that I can say for certain Angelo Marino is a big client. The bank statements you have prove that. Also, there are a few local politicians who use the firm. I'm sending you their names, though they're probably not the ones you're looking for. But I find it interesting. Also, Donovan was a client. I hacked NSWE's client database."

Jack laughed. "You're getting better."

Selena smiled, pleased with his praise. "I've been getting a lot of practice lately. I know I can count on you to keep me busy."

"Go ahead and send me the rest of what you dug up, then I want you to back off. These men mean business. And make sure you keep Ellis at your side."

"That's where he always is." Selena signed off.

"I thought you said she was a client?" John raised a brow at Jack.

"She is. She's also a valuable resource." Jack saved the files and patted Theo's hand, which still gripped his shoulder.

"So now what?" Theo took a seat in the chair next to Jack that John had vacated.

"I've got tails on Colm and Angelo. They'll report back if they see anything of interest. They'll keep records of everyone they come into contact with. We may get lucky."

John dropped into a chair, pulling Isabelle onto his lap. "If there's anything else I can do, let me know. And you two are welcome to stay here as long as you need. Isabelle and I have to get back to work tomorrow."

"I'll take Theo to the airport in the morning, and then I'll start digging further into NSWE. It probably will be a waste of time since Selena already looked into them, but I may find something she missed. And maybe I'll pay them a visit."

Theo shuddered but didn't say anything. She had to trust Jack knew what he was doing. She just didn't like that he was making himself a bigger target than he already was.

Theo spent the rest of the day sitting on the sidelines. Both Isabelle and John took a nap, their honeymoon finally catching up with them. Theo was tired but too wired to sleep. Jack was focused. Now that he had a solid lead, he was determined to find answers.

Theo went to bed early, but sleep didn't come. It was almost midnight when Jack came to her room. She had to be at the airport at nine, so she wasn't going to get much rest. When Jack slipped into bed beside her, Theo rolled over and leaned her head on his shoulder.

Jack wrapped his arm around her. "I was hoping you wouldn't mind my slipping in so late."

"I wasn't sleeping. But I wouldn't have minded either way." She pressed a kiss to his shoulder and snuggled closer.

Jack kissed the top of her head. "You will tell me as soon as you know, won't you?"

Theo closed her eyes, her voice a whisper. "Yes."

Jack relaxed. All day, thoughts of what could be between them teased his mind the moment he stopped focusing on the case. A baby would quickly change the dynamic of their relationship. Part of him hoped she was pregnant so she would be forced to choose to stay with him. He did not doubt that if she were pregnant, she wouldn't run off with his baby.

"It's not likely, Jack. And I'm sorry."

Jack scooted slightly away so he could see her face. "I'm not sorry, Theo, and I don't want you to be. We made that decision together. For better or for worse."

Vows. Theo wondered if she would ever hear those words in the context they were meant. She longed to hear them from Jack while standing at an altar. Years ago, she had thought she'd found the right man. Lying in bed with Jack, his arm wrapped around her, contentment filling her body simply by being beside him, she knew she hadn't known what love was all those years ago. Jack showed her that what she'd had before was a pale imitation of what love could be. She didn't know if Jack would ever love her, but he had already shown her more care than any other person had in her life.

To answer him, she simply nodded. The first time they had made love last night, it had been her choice. The second time had been his. She supposed they shared the responsibility.

Jack didn't try to make love to Theo; instead, he tucked her against him, closing his eyes. She had decided to go to the interview, and he had to respect that choice. Perhaps some distance was what the two of them needed. The circumstances under which they had started their relationship were not normal. When she was safe again and back to her old life, she might decide her work was more important than what they shared. He might love her, but she hadn't said anything to him that made him think she might love him back. He had told her he wanted her, wanted her for more than a day, a week, or a year. She hadn't responded. He hadn't asked her if he could make love to her that first time; he had simply taken her, and she had not denied him.

Within a few minutes of his joining her, he felt her snuggle down and fall asleep. He picked up his phone and set the alarm to wake them in plenty of time to get her to the airport. While she was safely tucked away for the next few days, he planned to find the man who attacked her and hopefully Donovan's murderer. He was glad Donovan was dead. From what he had learned about him during his brief investigation, the world was a better place without him. But his murder had, whether intentionally or accidentally, put Theo in danger. That was what he would do his best to solve.

The woman in his arms was hardly the type to inspire rage or revenge. She was the type of person who was nice to everyone she came in contact with. He wouldn't say she was naïve, but she was a caring person, and that trait stood out in her encounters with others. It was one of the things about her that attracted him. Even her career as a lawyer was a way for her to help other people. She helped people write their wills, buy a home, and make sure they were in good legal standing in their personal and business dealings.

So was this about Theo, or was she just handy? Did someone purposefully lure her to the office to find Donovan's body, or was it a coincidence? Those two questions remained unanswered. Jack wasn't a big believer in coincidence, given his line of work, but he just couldn't seem to figure out a motive for luring Theo there. She had already been slammed in the press, and her career was in ruins if revenge was the motive. And for someone like Theo, it was a very effective revenge. And if this were about drugs, Theo was as far removed from that world as anyone could be. Manufacturing evidence against her for murder would be more effort than it was worth, and most likely would not be effective. Anyone digging into Theo's life wouldn't believe she could murder someone the way Brandon Donovan had been murdered.

Sleep eluded Jack. When he was getting close to wrapping up a case, adrenaline kept him going. His mind was going a hundred miles a minute trying to arrange all that he'd learned over the last couple of days into a pattern. Something was missing, but he wasn't sure what. With Theo away, maybe he could focus and find the missing piece of the puzzle.

In the morning, Jack took Theo to the airport. He stayed with her until she passed the security checkpoint. He poured all of his feelings for her into their goodbye kiss, and it had both of them reeling. Theo's eyes were huge as they looked up at him. His were intense. Neither said anything, but before Theo turned from him, she hugged him tightly, tears glistening on her lashes.

Chapter Ten

"This was not how I planned to spend my evening." John yawned and leaned back into the passenger seat of Jack's car.

"You said you wanted to help. You're helping." Jack couldn't help but smile at John's sour look. Jack knew John had planned to spend the evening cuddled up next to his new wife. But Jack spoiled those plans when he told the couple he was going to stake out Colm's residence. Isabelle had insisted John go with Jack, just in case he needed backup.

"You don't need my help on a stakeout. You're just jealous that my lady is at home, and yours is a few hundred miles away." Despite his words, John kept the binoculars focused on the door of the dance club they were currently sitting outside of.

Knowing there was some truth to that, Jack suppressed a grin this time. "Hopefully Colm will get bored and go home. Then you can go home."

John snorted at that. "This guy gives new meaning to the word partying. He's visited seven clubs in the last four hours."

Jack was pretty sure he was inside selling drugs. Some of the names of the places they'd followed him to matched the names Theo remembered from Donovan's list. It was just more evidence that he was most likely the one who killed Donovan. It certainly looked like he had taken over his business.

Jack thought about going inside but had a feeling Colm knew exactly what he looked like. He considered sending in John, but given the violent nature of the murder and John's recent marriage, he wasn't going to put him in danger.

The two men watched the door for another twenty minutes when they finally hit pay dirt.

"Well, I'll be." Jack lifted his camera, zoomed in on his target, and snapped a few photos.

John perked up and scanned the doorway where Jack's camera was facing. "Who do we have here?"

"That would be Angelo Marino, Junior." Jack snapped another pic before setting the camera down. He opened the car door and started heading for the entrance.

John followed. "I thought you weren't going to make contact."

Jack paid the cover charge for the two of them, making sure to keep his distance. He slipped his cell phone out of his pocket and tapped the camera icon. "I wasn't going to, but I want proof of the two of them together."

John kept his back to Junior, blocking the man's view of Jack. Both men kept their distance from their quarry. Within a few moments of his arrival, Junior was seated across from Colm. Jack kept the phone low profile while he snapped a few pics. This was exactly what he had hoped to find. He also knew Junior's tail would be outside. Jack sent a text to the man to keep following Junior when he left the club.

Jack got a nice shot of drugs being passed from Colm to Junior. What interested him more was the envelope that he was sure consisted of a nice cash payment being handed from Junior to Colm. Given the size of the envelope, it contained more cash than the cost of those drugs accounted for.

Jack motioned for John to follow as the two men left the club. Jack sent another text, this one to the man tailing Colm. He wanted to keep tabs on him for the rest of the evening, but Jack had the shots he wanted. The next step was to take the photos and see if he could shake things up a bit.

Jack went straight to his laptop and uploaded the images once they were back at John's. He sent one file to Selena, one file to Tom, and the third file to Detective Mac Quinlan. Not surprisingly, Selena messaged him right away. Jack put her on video.

"You were busy tonight. What are your next steps?" Selena, still dressed in her cream linen suit even though it was midnight, couldn't stifle a yawn.

"I'm going to pay Angelo Senior a visit in the morning. Colm is the muscle, and probably not too bright. Angelo Junior seems to have gotten involved in the drug trade, and I'm guessing Angelo Senior knows all about it since he's the one holding the purse strings."

Selena looked around. "Where's Theo?"

"Out of town for the moment. What are you thinking?" Jack leaned back in the seat, contemplating the look on Selena's face.

"O'Carroll and Junior are about the same age. Given who their parents are, they probably move in the same social circles. Junior knows the law and how to circumvent it.

O'Carroll is the enforcer. O'Carroll did, for a time, have the funds, so in the early days, they wouldn't have needed Angelo Senior's money."

Jack followed her train of thought. "But with the cash gone in Colm's bank account, they might be looking for ways to enhance their cash flow. Maybe that's where the drugs play a role."

"Smuggling drugs is probably not that different from smuggling antiquities. We already know Angelo Senior is paying big bucks for stolen goods. Maybe the drugs are a side business and not the main focus of the smuggling, after all."

Jack considered that. "Regardless of which is the business's main bloodline, I know for a fact Donovan was heavily involved in the drug trade. Maybe getting rid of Donovan was a way to shift the focus back to smuggling antiquities."

Selena yawned again. "Follow the cash. It's rule number one, and it hardly ever fails."

Jack nodded and signed off. He had tons of bank statements. Colm's showed large withdrawals over the past year. His cash deposits were few and far between, hence the fact he went to Selena looking for cash. Angelo Senior's accounts showed large payments to NSWE. Junior's accounts showed not much activity at all. He certainly owed more than he was worth, but his accounts weren't any worse than most people's debts. He drove a flashy car he had bought with a high-interest loan; he wore nice clothes he paid for with plastic and lived beyond his means.

Unable to think straight any longer, Jack went to lay

down. He slept a little and was up once again before dawn. Around seven, he called Theo.

"You sound terrible, Jack. Did you get any sleep?" Theo fastened the earrings and straightened out the skirt Isabelle had chosen for the interview.

"Some. I got some pictures of Colm and Junior meeting in a club, exchanging drugs and cash." Jack leaned back, enjoying the sound of Theo's voice over the line.

"So maybe we've been focused on the wrong Angelo. I've been thinking about the attack, and the more I think about it, the more I'm convinced it was Colm. It's possible I recognized Colm from the office, but not because of his meetings with Angelo, but with Junior." Theo sat on the edge of the bed, wishing she were having this conversation in person.

"I talked to Selena last night, and she had the same thought. She pointed out that Colm and Junior could be part of the same social circle. It's not a stretch that the two of them went into business together. Junior is still not a partner at his family's firm, and I'm guessing there's a good reason why he's not. Daddy may be keeping him back."

"So is the next step questioning Angelo Senior?" Theo bit her lip to keep from asking him not to.

"Yeah. I've got some compromising pictures of his son. A little threat might go a long way toward getting the answers we want."

"Be careful, Jack. Whoever killed Donovan is dangerous."

"I promise you, Theo, I'll be in one piece when you get back. Call me later and tell me how the interview went."

"I will." Theo hung up the phone, her thoughts focused

solely on Jack and not the interview she was due for in an hour. Sighing, she fetched her jacket and left the hotel.

Jack set his cell phone down, worried about Theo's tone of voice. She had sounded remote. But he supposed, given the nature of their conversation, it was not surprising. What he wanted to do was call Theo back, tell her that he loved her, and to come home.

Jack showered and dressed, then drove out to Marino's law office. The drive took around an hour and a half. He parked his car in the garage and headed for the main lobby. He looked around, seeing a staircase that led to the executive suites. The same stairs Theo had used the night she discovered Donovan's body.

Jack climbed the stairs and smiled at the receptionist. "I'd like to see Angelo Marino."

The petite blonde gave him a flirtatious smile. "I'm afraid that Mr. Marino is not taking new clients right now."

Jack gazed at the door behind the blond. The lights were on. "I'm not here as a client. I'm here because I have something to discuss with him about Theodora Landry and his son, Angelo Junior. Call him."

The blonde was startled by Jack's harsh tone. She picked up the phone and relayed the message. Her eyes were scared when she told him to go in.

Jack didn't miss the fear or the fact that the receptionist immediately made herself unavailable. He opened the door to the office and closed it behind him. "Hello, Mr. Marino."

The older man stood, his gaze shuttered. "And who might you be?"

"Name's Jack Warner. But I'm guessing you know that

already." Jack took a step closer but didn't sit.

"I suppose I had an idea. Rumors are you're investigating Donovan's death. You should leave that to the police." Angelo, dressed in a very expensive, custom-made suit, sat back down behind his desk, his appearance that of a man with no worries.

"I'll tell you what I know. I know that your son is involved in the drug trade and that he was working with Brandon Donovan until his untimely death. I also know your son is hanging around Colm O'Carroll, a man guilty of smuggling antiquities. And I also know that you buy said antiquities from NSWE, owned by Colm. And the police know it as well."

Sweat broke out on Angelo's brow, but he was calm when he spoke. "I'm sure you're mistaken. I will admit my son is friends with Colm, an association I do not condone. As for my business dealings with NSWE, I have all the necessary paperwork claiming my legal right to ownership."

"I'm sure you do. So why don't you tell me why you fired Ms. Landry if you have nothing to hide? She brought you sufficient evidence that proved your CEO had illegal dealings with some very shady characters. Then within a few months, your CEO is dead, your son is caught on film exchanging drugs and cash, and Theo is threatened with physical harm if I don't stop my investigation."

"There was no proof in what she showed me that proved Donovan was guilty of any crimes. I had known him for years, and her allegations were outrageous. I can't have my employees spreading vicious rumors."

Jack rested his hands on the back of the chair, leaning

forward, meaning to intimidate. It wasn't hard to do at six-five. "I think you know exactly what Donovan was doing. I think you were helping him, using your firm as a cover for his illegal activities. And I think your son is involved."

Angelo sat completely still in his chair. "Prove it."

Jack pulled two color photos out of his breast pocket. One showed the transfer of drugs. One showed the transfer of cash. "These are currently in the hands of Detective Macaulay Quinlan. Who do you think will be pounding on your door next? Or your son's door?"

"I was being blackmailed into silence, and I can prove it." Angelo rose from his seat. "I admit I had an idea Donovan might be involved in a major drug ring, but I had no proof. My son had been hanging around Colm O'Carroll, and he had evidence that my son was not only using drugs but smuggling them. I, of course, didn't believe the evidence Donovan presented, but he made me keep quiet while he used my law firm as a cover for his smuggling. When Ms. Landry brought that package to my office, I panicked. I thought she would turn it over to the police. If she did that, Donovan would think I put her up to it. I fired her and had her removed. I destroyed the evidence. I threatened her with a libel suit to keep her quiet."

Jack's fingers tightened on the back of the chair. "Who killed Donovan? And who threatened Ms. Landry?"

"I don't know. It wasn't me. I had been keeping silent for so long; there was no reason for me to suddenly decide to have Donovan killed. As for Ms. Landry, she should stay out of it."

"Ms. Landry is out of it. You have to deal with me. But

don't worry, as I said, the detective should be beating a path to your door shortly." Jack pulled his phone out of his pocket. He made sure Angelo knew he had recorded the entire conversation and was still recording.

"You bastard. You don't know who you're dealing with." Angelo's temper flared.

"And who might that be? For the record, of course." Jack slipped the phone back into his pocket. Angelo didn't say another word.

Jack left the office and headed back to headquarters. With Theo out of town, he could go back to his office. He uploaded the sound file and sent it to Detective Quinlan. It wasn't much, but he at least had a motive for Donovan's murder. And if nothing else, the recording incriminated Angelo in covering up illegal drug smuggling. Jack hadn't heard anything back from the original detective investigating the murder, but Detective Quinlan could use the information to help find the man who attacked Theo and then share the evidence with the other detective. Detective Quinlan would have the right resources to track down the names of the drug traffickers involved, and he seemed willing to go above and beyond. While Jack normally would have pursued it himself, right now he needed to focus on Theo. It wasn't drug runners who were after her. It was someone closer than that.

One thing was nagging at him. In the office, Angelo had said he had no reason for having Donovan killed. He hadn't said he had no reason to kill him. So either Angelo ordered the hit, or he knew who had. Jack typed up his notes and sent those off to the detective as well. Detective Quinlan might not be thrilled with him and what most police termed "interference," but with Theo's safety as his top priority, he wasn't worried about ruffling the detective's feathers.

It was after lunch when Theo called. Jack set aside the sandwich he was eating and answered her call. There was only one thing he wanted to know. "How did it go?"

Theo wasn't sure if she should be pleased or upset. "The interview went very well. They are looking for someone with a background in estate planning, which I've done a significant amount of. The man who interviewed me was impressed with my role at Marino Law Firm. He was also impressed with my education and previous internship work. He said they would be deciding before the week was out, but that I was one of the most qualified applicants they'd met. And he said there was no need for a second interview. I was a last-minute interview for them. They had already done a couple of rounds with other applicants."

"So soon? I'm glad to hear it went well. They would be foolish not to hire you. I take it you didn't mention you'd been fired or why." Jack tossed his lunch in the trash, no longer hungry.

"They didn't ask, and I didn't offer the information. I don't know if they would have cared; I checked off most of the boxes on the job description. Jack, we need to talk about this."

"I know. We can talk about it when you get back. Right now I'm up to my eyebrows in evidence, trying to tie it all together. I visited Angelo Senior today, and he was downright chatty. He admitted he knew what Donovan was doing, but he claimed he was being blackmailed with false evidence against his son. I recorded the conversation and turned it over to the detective. By now, I imagine the police have a search warrant for both the Marinos."

"Did he mention Colm? Did he say who killed Donovan?" Theo asked.

"He only said Colm and his son were friends, and that he didn't approve of their friendship. He said he didn't know who had Donovan killed. Nothing else for now. What time does your flight get in tomorrow?"

Theo sighed and didn't push him for any more information. "I'll be late. The flight should arrive around eight. I'll text you and meet you at the main entrance."

"I can come in and find you." Jack closed his eyes, trying to picture Theo lying on the hotel bed. Then his mind started imagining all sorts of other things.

"Don't worry about it. I just have one piece of luggage. It will be easier if you don't have to park."

"All right. I'll be waiting. So, what are you wearing?" Jack grinned at the ceiling when Theo giggled, as he had hoped.

"Seriously, Jack. You're incorrigible."

"Yeah, but I'm cute, and you love it." Jack propped his feet on his desk, enjoying the banter.

"I do, Jack." Theo's tone went soft.

Jack dropped his feet to the floor, his heart pounding. "Say it, Theo."

Theo's voice was barely a whisper. "Not until you ask me to stay."

Jack was quiet for a moment. "I told you I wanted you to stay, but I can't make this choice for you."

And that was the problem. Theo needed Jack to ask her to stay without a "but" attached. She wanted to stay, but she wanted to know he needed her as much as she needed him. He wanted her to tell him she loved him. But she couldn't do that until he made a real commitment to her. She needed to know that she was what he wanted and that he was willing to do what it took to keep her.

"We'll talk about this later. I should get back to work." Jack kept Theo on the line for a few more minutes before hanging up. Jack rubbed his temples. He should have told her he loved her. He had demanded she tell him, but she had balked. Not that he could blame her. Her father hadn't made a real commitment to any woman in his life, including his daughter. Theo's fiancé left her to marry another woman. He knew she had insecurities. Hadn't her vulnerability been one of the things that attracted him? No doubt she needed him to step up and bare his soul first before she would hers. He supposed what bothered him was he didn't want to make this decision for her. He wanted her to choose him without his asking.

Jack dragged himself away from thoughts of Theo and went back to work. If Angelo had paid someone to kill Donovan, there had to be a trail. If he went with the premise that Colm was a man for hire, then it was his accounts he needed to track. He thought of calling Selena, but he meant what he said about her staying out of it. He could bug Tom but had a feeling he was going to be too distracted to be of much use. He knew from a conversation earlier in the day that he and Tiffany were writing out invitations for their wedding later tonight.

Knowing he needed help, Jack dialed Detective Quinlan. "How far have you gotten tracking Colm's accounts?"

Mac scowled at the phone, but he had to admit Jack had been forthcoming with all the evidence he had found since the beginning of the investigation. Detective Lowell from the city over wasn't happy with him investigating Donovan's murder, but the man also didn't seem to mind turning his work over to someone else. Mac had done all the legwork since Theo's attack. "I've been having our team run searches since you sent me your notes this afternoon. I'm happy to say we found an offshore account for Colm O'Carroll. And I also have to say that I'm pretty sure Angelo Marino Senior paid to have Brandon Donovan murdered. I believe the man he paid was Colm O'Carroll. And Angelo Marino Junior is involved with some shady dealers, of both the antiquity and drug variety. Detective Lowell has warrants for all three of their arrests as we speak. I've got one of my own on Colm O'Carroll for the attack on Ms. Landry. Marino Senior is already in custody. He's been singing like a bird, doing what he can to cut a deal. He's even willing to sell out his son. He's one of the best defense attorneys in the state. He knows how to play the game. He'll end up in prison for his crimes, but he's already in the process of cutting a deal to reduce his sentence."

"And Colm?" Jack sent another text to the man following Colm. He'd been messaging his man on and off for the last two hours with no response.

"He's gone to ground. He's not home, he's not at any of his offices, and he's not at his usual haunts. I don't suppose you know where he is?"

Jack swore under his breath. "I don't. I had a tail on Colm, but so far, I haven't heard back from him. I'm going to try to hunt down my man. And the tail I had on Junior lost him and is now sitting outside the man's house. There's been no activity there. I'll get back to you."

Mac cursed. "I'm not too worried about Junior. He'll turn up. It's Colm I'm worried about. He has quite the rap sheet. And if he's a hitman, you'd better pray he didn't notice your guy following him. Call me as soon as you find him."

Jack hung up and pulled up the GPS tracker on Anthony's car, the man he had tailing Colm, and saw that it was parked behind a nightclub in a seedy part of town. It hadn't moved in over an hour. Jack tucked his weapon into his holster while heading to Tom's office.

Tom was behind his desk going over reports when Jack burst in. "What's happened?"

"Anthony is not responding. I have his car across town. He was tailing O'Carroll. I need backup."

Tom went to his safe and pulled his weapon out. He rarely had reason to use it these days and was excited by the prospect. "Let's go."

Both men were quiet on the drive over. Tom kept an eye out for a tail, while Jack broke a few traffic laws. Anthony's car was parked behind a dumpster. Tom kept vigil beside the car, keeping an eye on the parking lot and side alley. Jack approached the car from behind, keeping an eye out as well. When he got to the car, he peeked through the back window. His oath was loud and echoed through the alley. Anthony was in the car, all right, but he wasn't moving.

"We need an ambulance." Jack shouted to Tom, yanking

on the car door. When it wouldn't open, he used his pistol to break the window. He quickly unlocked the door and checked Anthony for a pulse. A wave of relief poured through him when he felt it. It was weak, but it was there. The man was unconscious but alive.

Jack stayed with Anthony while Tom kept an eye out for trouble. The ambulance arrived within fifteen minutes. Anthony had taken a bullet in the shoulder and another in his side. From what the paramedics could tell, the bullet hadn't struck any vital organs. Tom had already called Detective Quinlan, and the man said he was on his way. Other local police officers arrived only a moment behind the ambulance. The crime scene was quickly taped off, and evidence was being gathered. Jack and Tom agreed to follow the ambulance back to the hospital. Tom called Anthony's emergency contact, which ended up being his sister.

Surgery was performed to remove the two bullets, and within a few short hours, Anthony was sedated and in bed. It was another hour before he woke.

"I'm sorry, Mr. Warner. I didn't know he was behind me until it was too late. He must have made me."

"Who shot you, Anthony?" Jack set his phone on the table to record the meeting for the detective. Mac had come and gone while Anthony was in surgery.

"It was Colm, sir. I got a good look at him in the side mirror right before he shot me."

Tom spoke. "He probably knew the cops were looking for him. Angelo's arrest made the afternoon news. Police departments can't keep a secret, especially when it involves multiple jurisdictions. Detective Quinlan should be back soon to take your statement. Security cameras in the parking lot didn't work, so we don't have the shooting on camera. The detective went out to the crime scene to look it over."

"I'll have a guard put outside the door. Hopefully, we can keep the fact that Anthony's alive a secret until we track Colm down." Jack looked at Anthony. "Right now you're our only witness that Colm is a killer."

"Yes, sir." Anthony's voice faded as he drifted back to sleep.

"Detective Quinlan will have all his men on the lookout for Colm." Jack strode down the hall, heading back to his vehicle.

"I'll have our men start doing a sweep as well. He's bound to surface." Tom climbed into the passenger seat. He knew that look on Jack's face. He was on a mission to find a killer. It's why he wanted Jack, and no one else, guarding his daughter.

"I'm supposed to pick Theo up at the airport tomorrow night. I think I'll stash her at the office. Right now that's the safest place for her. I'll have Isabelle pack her a bag, and I'll take it back to the office."

"We'll find him, Jack, and put him away for good." Tom spoke, hoping to calm Jack down. Tom wanted to find the man and tear him apart for hurting his daughter, so he knew what Jack was feeling. But revenge couldn't be taken, and the law had to be followed. Both men understood that.

Jack took a deep breath. "We'll find him. But don't plan on him going down easy. Colm has proven he's ruthless, and he'll do what he can to stay out of prison."

Both men considered that fact. Tom knew Jack was right. Colm probably would not go down without a fight. He looked forward to it.

Chapter Eleven

The night passed with no sightings of Colm. He hadn't used his credit card, hadn't pulled cash from an ATM, or even bought dinner, nothing they were able to trace. Jack had every investigator looking for a lead. Detective Quinlan was back at the precinct, using all the resources at his disposal to find him.

Jack slammed his fist on the table. "Still nothing. I've got to pick Theo up in a few hours, and we're no closer to locating this bastard than we were yesterday."

Tom yawned. "He'll eventually make a mistake. Men like him always do. We'll set Theo up here, like you said, until he's found. There's a major manhunt for him; he won't be able to hide forever."

He could keep her here, but she wouldn't be thrilled. At some point, she might just decide it wasn't worth it and take the job if it was offered. She would certainly be safer a few hundred miles away until Colm was found. A different fear settled into his stomach. He couldn't let Theo go. He wouldn't let her go.

"You look like you had an epiphany, Jack." Tom yawned again. He wasn't used to all-nighters anymore, and the night had long since passed.

"I'm in love with Theo." Jack almost sighed in relief that he had said it.

"That's not exactly an epiphany, Jack. I've known that for the past three months. I hope you plan on forgetting this nonsense about letting her leave."

Jack glanced at Tom but figured he shouldn't be surprised. The guy was one of the best investigators he'd ever met. "I'm not letting her leave. The problem is what she'll do for work. She doesn't want to keep working for you."

"Truth be told, I don't want her to. I don't have much use for an attorney who specializes in estate planning. She's been nagging me about writing a will. And now, with the baby coming, she'll be on me even more."

"Just do as she asks. It will be easier that way." Jack thought about what he had said and knew that he needed to take that same advice.

"I suppose I will. I'll have her help me with that when I get back from my honeymoon. Don't want to jinx it."

Jack laughed. Trust Tom to joke about dying before his nuptials. "You'll have to wait until she gets back from hers. I'm tired of pussyfooting around and playing games. As soon as Colm is in jail, I plan on flying her to Vegas."

Tom laughed. "That's very tacky, Jack, but she might just go for it."

"I'm planning on it." Jack rubbed his tired eyes. "I need to close my eyes before I pick up Theo. I can't see straight to drive."

Jack left Tom in his office and headed back to his own. He set his cell phone on the table and stretched out on the couch. It had been almost twenty-four hours since he'd slept last, and even then, it had only been a few hours. He'd be no good to Theo dead on his feet.

Jack had been asleep for a couple of hours when his phone buzzed. Still half asleep, Jack checked to see who texted him. Within a moment, he was alert and awake. Selena had sent him a 911.

"What is it?" Jack didn't bother with pleasantries.

"I had Wallace set up an alert on both you and Theo, should anyone try to gain access to any digital information about you. I just got a notice that someone hacked into Theo's flight schedule. Whoever it was, they know when Theo lands."

Jack cursed and ran out of the office. "Thanks, I owe you."

"You'd do the same for me." Selena hung up.

Tom was dozing when Jack barged in. "What?"

"Colm is going to try to grab Theo at the airport. Call Detective Quinlan." Jack grabbed the jacket and holster he had left in Tom's office. He watched impatiently as Tom phoned the detective. He then rushed from the room. He wanted to find Colm before he found Theo.

Tom was right beside him. "I'll get a few men headed toward the airport. The detective will put out an alert with airport security. Hopefully, they'll trace him quickly."

Mac was already at the airport when they arrived. "I've got men sweeping the airport now. They're dressed like civilians, so they won't be as easily detected. So far, no one has seen him. I don't want him to get suspicious and take off."

The detective got them through security. "Theo doesn't know what's going on. I need to be at her gate and get her away from here as soon as possible. I don't want Colm getting within a thousand feet of her."

Tom and the detective did their best to blend in with the crowd. Mac monitored the area outside the terminal. Tom stood to the side of the terminal where Theo was due to arrive in the next fifteen minutes, and so far, he hadn't seen a sign of Colm in the past couple of hours they had been at the airport. It would be expected that, should anyone be watching, Jack would retrieve Theo, so Tom wasn't worried about Jack being seen.

Jack had an earbud in and was listening to the police band. So far, no one else had spotted him either. He looked over at Tom, who shook his head. Tom was listening to his team that was sweeping the airport.

Theo's flight was on time, and he waited to the side for the passengers to deplane. Theo stepped out, and Jack stepped forward.

"Jack." Theo smiled at him, happy to see him. "I told you that you didn't have to come in."

Jack embraced Theo and used his hold on her to pull her to the side. Most people would see a couple reunited. He knew Theo felt the tension in him. "Colm might be at the airport. Someone hacked your flight schedule."

Theo shuddered. "What do we do?"

Jack kissed her briefly, then started pulling her toward the terminal exit. "Cops and investigators are swarming the airport looking for him. I'm taking you back to headquarters where you'll stay until Colm is found. Angelo Senior was arrested this afternoon."

Theo glanced around and saw her father. Then she saw

the man behind him. "Jack."

Jack looked up and saw Colm standing behind Tom. Tom was standing completely still. Colm smiled at him and gestured with his free hand. Jack looked around and didn't see the detective. He discreetly opened the comm line on the walkie-talkie in his coat pocket.

Jack set Theo behind him, keeping her hand in his as he approached Colm. There were dozens of men looking for the man. One was bound to notice. "You're making a big mistake."

Colm discreetly showed Jack his gun, then pushed it back into Tom's back. "How did you know I was here?"

"A little bird told me." Jack kept his eyes on Colm's. He could feel Theo trembling against him.

"The four of us are going to take a walk. My car is parked just outside the maintenance entrance." Colm pushed Tom in the direction he wanted them to go. Jack kept his distance and Theo behind him. Both he and Tom were armed. All he needed was a distraction.

Colm turned his cold eyes on Theo. "I warned you to call off your investigator. You should have listened to me."

Theo kept her eyes on Jack and ignored his taunt. "You killed Donovan."

Colm laughed. "As to that, I didn't want to, but I couldn't resist. Angelo Senior was being blackmailed by Donovan, or so he thought, and wanted Donovan permanently out of his life. He offered me quite a large sum to take him out. I tried to make it look like a cartel killed him, and I did a damn good job. Little did Marino know I was the one who had convinced Donovan to blackmail him in the first place. I was the one who gathered the evidence against Junior. It was easy enough since Junior was working for me. Once Donovan was out of the picture, that left Junior and me to run the show. It was quite amusing that dear old Daddy paid the man responsible for blackmailing him to kill the messenger."

Tom kept walking but turned to look at Colm. "You have lost it, haven't you? Your father must be spinning in his grave."

"My dear old daddy was weak. He should have kept out of my affairs. The antiquities business was the perfect cover for smuggling drugs. Much to my surprise, there was even more money in smuggling antiquities. When the Feds caught on to my plan, it was easy enough to blame my father for it. But the authorities didn't do their job. Said there wasn't enough evidence. He should have gone to jail. Instead, he apologized and returned the artifacts. Daddy had to go."

They reached the maintenance section, and Colm waved them toward the exit. He looked at Theo. "Open the door."

Theo glanced at Jack, who nodded. Theo slowly opened the door and cringed when an alarm went off.

"Move it." Colm shoved Tom out the door and then turned his gun on Jack.

Colm waved the trio toward a service van parked a few feet away. "We're going for a ride."

Junior jumped out of the driver's seat. "Took long enough. We need to get out of here."

Theo wasn't sure what happened next. She felt Jack shove her to the ground. She thought she heard shouting from the other side of the van. Shots were fired over her head. She heard Jack grunt, but he remained standing. She looked up and saw him fire his weapon.

A few more shots rang out, and then it was quiet. She felt Jack lift her to her feet, pressing her face to his chest. She tried to pull away, but his strong grip kept her against him. Instead of fighting him, she wound her arms around his waist and held on.

"Get her out of here." Jack kissed Theo roughly and handed her to her father. Tom tugged her hand and quickly led her away. She saw Jack heading toward Detective Quinlan, who was standing over Colm's body. She started to protest, but her father dragged her out of view so she wouldn't see Colm.

Jack turned to see Tom pulling his daughter back inside the airport. He didn't want her to see this. He glanced over at Colm's body. It was his shot to the heart that killed him. Mac looked over at Angelo Junior, who was now in custody. He had dropped his weapon and had thrown himself inside the van when the first shot rang.

"Nice shot." Mac kicked the gun away from Colm's hand. A junior officer came and collected it. "He could have killed you."

Jack nodded. Colm had swung around, and whether by choice or by circumstance, he had aimed his weapon at Theo. The detective had told him to drop his weapon, but Colm's eyes told Jack there was no chance of that. Without a second thought, Jack fired. "He was going to kill Theo."

"I know. I'll still need to bring you in, but it was a justified shooting. The DA will have my testimony to that fact. And you sure are handy with recordings. We have Colm's confession on file. And I have no doubt both Angelo Marinos will spill their guts." Mac took Jack's arm, and Jack didn't resist.

Jack, however, did wince. Both men looked down. There was blood on his jacket.

Mac cursed. "Why didn't you tell me you were shot?"

"Didn't know." Jack's arm started to hurt. He watched somewhat detached as the detective called over a paramedic.

The bullet had only grazed him, and the paramedic patched him up. Jack refused pain medication and refused to go to the hospital. He looked up when Theo came rushing toward him.

"You scared ten years off my life." Theo threw herself into Jack's arms. His arms went around her. He noticed Colm's body was covered so Theo wouldn't see the bloody mess. She had seen enough death already. He knew the instant Theo saw the bandage on his arm. She turned completely white.

"I'm fine. Just a graze." Jack tucked a finger under Theo's chin and lifted her head to his. He kissed her roughly. He didn't care that they had an audience. He needed a taste of her before Mac hauled him to the police station.

Theo moaned and wrapped her arms around Jack's neck. She didn't want to let him go.

Mac cleared his throat. "You'll have plenty of time for that later; I promise."

Jack set Theo from him. He nodded to Tom, who once again came to Theo's side. Tom wrapped an arm around his daughter's waist.

Theo felt tears fall as she watched the detective take Jack away. She knew Jack was not under arrest, at least not yet. But she couldn't help the fear that pervaded her.

"He'll be fine. It was a justified shooting. Jack has a license to carry that gun. There will be an investigation, but everything will be just fine. We'll go back to my house and wait for Jack."

Theo let her father lead her back through the airport and to the car he and Jack had driven there. She needed her father's strength right now. She needed to believe him when he said everything was going to be fine.

* * *

Theo was pacing her father's home office. Jack had called to tell her that he had been released and would be at the house shortly. It was well after midnight, but Theo didn't feel even the slightest bit tired. She wanted to see Jack.

She had let herself be driven back to her father's house. On the way there, she had called Isabelle and told her what happened. Isabelle relayed the message to John, who then relayed a message to Selena. Since there was nothing else to do, Theo let her father take over from there.

Her father had even gotten her to eat a light snack that his housekeeper fixed for her. She was now sipping a cup of hot decaf coffee, lightly laced with the whiskey her father kept stashed in his desk. Even the alcohol couldn't calm her.

Theo was the first to hear Jack's voice shout hello through the house. Theo ran out of her father's office and met Jack in the hall. Jack caught Theo in his arms. He felt her hot tears soak the front of his shirt. He felt his eyes sting. He lifted Theo into his arms. He saw Tom in his office doorway, and he carried her back there. He sat on the couch, keeping Theo in his arms. She had buried her face in his chest, and she didn't look like she planned to move.

"What did the detective say?" Tom poured Jack a shot of whiskey and handed it to him.

"He said he was sure they had a clean case against Colm and the Marinos. Junior lawyered up and is keeping his mouth shut for now. Doesn't matter. Senior already admitted to hiring Colm and was willing to turn over the evidence Donovan had given him against his son. If Junior's smart, he'll spill his guts. Now that Colm's bank account was traced, the cops will use that account to find out where the money came from. Within the week, the cops should have all the evidence they need, along with the drug dealer's and smuggler's names Junior and Colm were working with."

Tom took a large swallow of his whiskey. "Was it on purpose or by accident that Theo found Donovan's body?"

Jack set his glass down. "Accident. Colm admitted he wanted it to look like drug dealers killed him. It wasn't his intention to point the blame at Theo. My theory is that Donovan asked Theo to the office, most likely to buy her off. He was blackmailing his boss, was dealing drugs, and probably figured paying Theo off and getting Angelo to drop the libel suit was the easiest route to keeping his activities secret. When Angelo went to the press and told the public he was bringing libel charges against Theo for slandering his CEO, Donovan was likely concerned about all the media attention the lawsuit was getting. The last thing he wanted was someone becoming curious and looking closer into her allegations. He was probably worried she'd go to the press and defend herself."

Theo finally lifted her head. She was oddly relieved to know her finding Donovan's body was not intentional. But she was still worried about Jack and tightened her arms around him. "You won't be arrested?"

Jack kissed her brow. "No. Detective Quinlan saw Colm aim at you. If I hadn't taken the shot, Mac would have."

Shock kept Theo silent. Jack had saved her life, and she hadn't known it. She never saw Colm aim his gun at her because Jack had done his best to keep himself between her and Colm. She shuddered, then tucked her head back against Jack's chest.

"I think we all need some rest." Tom finished his whiskey and left the office.

Jack stood and set Theo on her feet. Her eyes were red from her tears, but she had never looked sexier. "Where's your room?"

Theo laughed. "It's at the top of the stairs."

"How far away is it from your father's room?"

Theo looked up, realized why he was asking, then blushed. "Far enough."

It took Jack all of thirty seconds to strip off his clothes once he got her bedroom door closed behind them. It only took him another thirty to strip Theo's clothes off. Jack tumbled her to the bed. When her thighs opened to him, he slid deep inside her body. He felt the slight resistance of her body to the sudden intrusion, but she took him easily. He lay on her, content now that he had her beneath him.

There was no urgency to their lovemaking. Jack kissed Theo deeply, repeatedly, his tongue mimicking the movements of his body inside hers. He took her slowly and let her climax build. When it came, he followed her over the edge.

It didn't escape either of their notice that he had made love to her again without protection. Jack rolled from her body and settled her against him.

Theo sat up, clutching the sheet to her chest. "Jack. We need to talk."

Jack looked up at Theo. Her hair was in tangles around her face, and her lips were swollen from his. He caressed her cleavage above the sheet, unable to keep his hands off her. "I didn't give you the right answer on the phone."

Theo let the sheet fall to her waist. "Ask me to, Jack."

Jack sat up and twisted his body toward her. "Stay."

Theo felt new tears sting her eyes, but these were happy tears. "I love you, Jack."

Jack kissed her again, crushing her body against his. He rolled them over, pressing her onto the bed. "I love you, Theo. I've wanted to tell you for so long."

Theo's brows shot up in surprise. "For how long?"

Jack kissed her. "Forever."

Epilogue

Theo glanced around the main area of her new office, admiring the finished result. Jack had solved her employment problem by convincing her to go into business for herself. Her father had seconded the idea. She wasn't sure she should be pleased with how they were conspiring together, but since it was to make her happy, she decided it wasn't such a bad thing.

She was now the proud owner of her own law firm, specializing in estate planning, wills, and trusts. Her father was going to be her first client, though he grumbled a bit about it. Jack and her father had suggested she go into business before she had gotten a call back about her interview. They had enthusiastically given her the job, which pleased Theo immensely. However, she had politely declined and started looking for the perfect office space while she navigated her way around setting up a new business enterprise.

It was a lovely space, nicer than she might have rented on her own. Jack and her father had told her there was space available in the same building their office occupied. Her father had given her the down payment to rent the space before she had even agreed to move into it. Jack then seconded the idea. After what they had been through, she knew Jack liked the idea of having her nearby.

Once she had signed the lease, she enlisted the help of Isabelle to decorate. Not only did Isabelle have great taste in clothes, as her new wardrobe attested to, she also had great taste in furniture. They had spent hours poring over fabric samples, artwork, and furniture while laying out the design of what was now her beautiful new space.

Theo glanced up at Jack, who had enlisted John's help moving in the last of the furniture. The office space held two rooms. The main office held a reception area, with a cozy sitting area for clients. She and Jack had finished setting it up yesterday. Isabelle had filled it with watercolors and overstuffed chairs. Her personal office space held a large antique desk, a gift from Selena, a couple of bookcases that now held her law books, and a large comfy couch. The desk took both men lifting and carrying it to get it inside.

"The room is just perfect." Theo glanced over at Isabelle. "I can't thank you enough."

Isabelle simply smiled. "I can't wait to help you decorate your nursery. Now that is going to be fun."

Theo's hand went to her stomach. Jack had made good on his word to her father and had whisked her off to Vegas. She had packed the silver dress she had bought for her father's wedding, and it had been perfect for her own. Jack had kissed her tenderly after zipping her into it, his fingers stroking the skin the dress exposed. With Jack dressed in a dark suit, they had stood in the not-as-tacky-as-expected wedding chapel and said their vows. Jack's calm voice vowed for better or for worse. Vows she had dreamed of hearing him say to her one day. She returned those vows wholeheartedly.

She had been disappointed when her period had come a few days after their hasty wedding. But a few short weeks after it ended, she started to feel queasy. She had already known she was pregnant when she missed her period. She and Jack had stopped using birth control altogether since that first time. As soon as she started to feel ill, she told Jack. He had her make an appointment with her doctor, who confirmed she was indeed pregnant. They decided to wait a couple of months before telling her father. She wanted to see him married first.

Her father's wedding to Tiffany took place two months after hers and Jack's, and they still hadn't told her father. Theo and Jack had then decided to wait a little while before announcing the pregnancy to their friends and family. In the end, Tiffany gave birth before they told them. Their son, William Theodore Landry, was born a couple of weeks early but healthy.

"Selena wants to help with the nursery since she couldn't help with the office. She's threatened bodily harm if we don't let her." Theo had become friends with Selena over the past few weeks. The woman, who at first had seemed cold and distant, had proven otherwise. Theo realized she was simply reserved. Isabelle was already friends with Selena since the other woman was such a large donor to The Heart's Way Foundation. Isabelle had now gotten Theo on board, helping with various fundraisers. The three women spent a lot of time together. Theo doubted she'd have much time, or money, to invest in the foundation now that her business was almost up and running, but it felt good to help while she could.

Isabelle nodded while fluffing a pillow. "She's as excited as I am. I'm not quite ready to have a baby myself. Your baby will give me practice before John and I have our own. Selena swears she'll never get married again, but I hope that isn't true."

Theo and Isabelle made a few slight adjustments to the room before going to find their men. There was a lot of grunting and groaning going on as they wrestled with the last of the furniture.

Isabelle and John left shortly after the desk was set up. Jack was sweating a little from the effort it took to get the desk situated in the room, but he was looking pleased. Theo glanced around her now completed office. Isabelle had hung the artwork yesterday, while Theo had filled the bookcases that were already in place.

"What do you think, Mrs. Warner?" Jack came up behind her and wrapped his arms around her, his hands resting on her ever-so-slightly swollen belly.

"It's perfect. I couldn't have done this without you. I never would have thought to open my own business." Theo rested her hands on top of Jack's.

Jack spun Theo in his arms, lifting her and setting her on the desk. Desire darkened his eyes. "I love you, Theodora."

Theo's thighs clasped around Jack, her arms bringing him closer, her love for him shining in her eyes. "I love you, Jack."

Jack's hands went to the hem of her skirt, and he showed her how much right there on her new desk.

<u>From The Author</u>

I hope you enjoyed the second book in my series, The Heart's Way. All books in the series can be read alone, but I think it's more fun to read them in order. If you missed the first book, For Now and Always, you can pick up your copy, as well as books 3 and 4, Say You Love Me and Forever Love.

If you enjoyed the book and would like an email on my next release, please sign up for my newsletter @ elizabeth-castle.com/contact. Please be assured that your email will never be sold (I wouldn't want mine sold, so I wouldn't do that to someone else). You can also follow me on Facebook @ facebook.com/elizabethcastle.romanceauthor

Also, if you enjoyed this book, or any of my other titles, please consider leaving a rating at your favorite retailer, Goodreads and/or Bookbub. And if you have the time, a text review would be lovely. Indie authors rely on readers like you to tell others how much you enjoy their books.

Happy Reading,

Lizzy Castle

Books by Elizabeth Castle

Single Titles:
  Going Home
  This Kind Of Love
  Chasing Hope
  The Babe & The Librarian (novella)

The Heart's Way
Series:
  For Now and
Always
  Ask Me To
  Say You Love Me
  Forever Love

Bennett Family Series:
  This Time Love
  A Bride For David
(novella)

All Of Me Series:
  All Of My Days
  All Of My Nights

Cantwell Quartet
Series:
  Falling Slowly
  Unraveled
  Hidden Away
  Entangled

Contemporary "Retro" Romance Series:
  Loving Jordan

Visit elizabeth-castle.com for newsletter sign up and up-to-date releases.

www.ingramcontent.com/pod-product-compliance
Lightning Source LLC
Chambersburg PA
CBHW020802310726
48969CB00002B/667